ACCIDENTALLY
Friends

candy apple books...
just for you.
sweet. fresh. fun.
take a bite!

by Lisa Papademetriou

SCHOLASTIC INC.

New York   Toronto   London   Auckland   Sydney
Mexico City   New Delhi   Hong Kong   Buenos Aires

To Anamika Bhatnagar, who accidentally became my editor . . . and friend

ISBN-13: 978-0-545-04670-1
ISBN-10: 0-545-04670-X

12 11 10 9 8 7 6 5 4 3   9 10 11 12 13 14/0
Printed in the U.S.A.

First printing, July 2009

CHAPTER ONE

Amy's Wedding Rule: Everyone has parents. Try not to freak out if they start dancing.

"Do you think anyone would notice if I just ducked under the table?" My good friend, Jenelle Renwick, toyed with the edge of the white linen tablecloth. "I could just hang out here until the band stops playing."

I grinned. "Can't deal with your mom doing the Funky Waggle?" The Waggle was a dance craze that must have swept the country about thirty years ago, because all of our parents seemed to know it. My mom and dad were on the dance floor, too. My brother, Kirk, was standing near them, snapping photos with his new digital camera. I was pretty sure he'd try to use them as blackmail later.

"I'm not sure who's worse," Jenelle admitted. "Mom or Great-uncle Norman."

Jenelle glanced to one end of the dance floor, where a heavyset man with a red face was shaking his hips and letting out excited whoops in time to the beat. Jenelle's mom, Linda, was at the center of the floor in her elegant ivory wedding gown. She and my uncle Steve were laughing and dancing. Actually, Linda and Steve were decent dancers. I didn't think Jenelle had too much to be embarrassed about.

"They look like they're having the time of their lives," I said, half to myself.

"Amy Flowers, are you serious?" Jenelle demanded, sliding her fork through the moist slice of white cake on the delicate china plate in front of her. "They look like mental patients!" She was smiling when she said it, and I could tell that she thought her mom and Steve were cute.

A handsome man with silver hair cut in on Uncle Steve. "Who's that guy?" I asked as Linda laughed and Funky Waggled off with her new partner.

Jenelle's fork paused halfway to her lips. "My dad," she said. She placed her fork back on her plate. Her face was as still as a quiet lake as she looked out at the dance floor. Jenelle was wearing a rose-colored chiffon dress, and with her blond waves loose around her face, she looked like an ancient oil painting in a museum.

I touched her shoulder. "Are you okay?" I asked. I knew that Jenelle's mother and father were still friendly — even though they were divorced — so I wasn't surprised that he was at the wedding.

Jenelle gave her head a quick shake, as if she was clearing her mind. "I'm fine," she said, and smiled at me. The smile was sad — but just a little. She looked out at the dance floor again, where Uncle Steve had just pulled Jenelle's grandmother into the party. "Steve is great. And I know Mom is crazy about him."

"But he's not your dad," I said.

Jenelle turned and looked at me with large hazel eyes. "Yeah," she said simply. She sighed and took a bite of the cake. I'd already finished mine. I'd really had to restrain myself from picking up the plate and licking it in front of everyone — it was that good. But it was a pretty fancy party, so I held back.

I sneaked a glance over toward the long table by the back of the room, where a large punch bowl was set up. Beside it was a huge display of chocolate cupcakes topped with elaborate frosted sunflowers. This was the groom's cake, and at the end of the night everyone would receive a box with a cupcake in it as a party favor. If the cupcakes were half as good as the cake, they would probably be the best party favors in the history of the known universe.

"More iced tea?" asked a voice.

"Definitely!" It was some "peach-mango infusion" thing and just about the best drink I'd ever had. I held out my glass, and the busboy winked a chocolatey brown eye at me. My mouth fell open. "Scott?" I nearly dropped my glass in surprise.

"Whoa — steady," he said. "Don't want this to end up all over your dress."

"What — what are you doing here?" I asked as I tried to get a grip — in more ways than one. It was taking a long time for me to process what was going on. Scott Lawton, my crush from Allington Academy, was here. He was a busboy at my friend's mom's wedding. He was serving me peach-mango iced tea. For a brief moment, I wondered if I was on hidden camera or something.

Scott shrugged. "My dad has some pretty strict ideas about allowances and stuff. As in — he won't give me one. He's had a job since he was eleven, so he thinks everyone else should, too. My mom hooked me up with this catering job. A friend of hers owns the company."

"Can't your dad give you a job at his company?" I asked. Scott's father owns a super-cool video game company.

Scott grinned, revealing his perfect teeth. I couldn't help noticing how cute he was in his long white apron. "Dad says he'll give me an internship when I'm a senior in high school, but only if I prove myself," Scott said. "And it'll be unpaid, anyway, so I'll still have to work somewhere else if I want spending money."

"Your dad is seriously tough." Jenelle looked impressed.

I was kind of impressed, too. The school we went to was one of the most exclusive private academies in Texas, and many of the Allington parents acted like glorified cash machines. Not my parents, though. I was on a scholarship. We weren't poor, but I didn't roll up to school in a chauffeur-driven limo, either, like half of my classmates.

"He's strict about some things," Scott admitted. "So, hey, are you guys excited about Crazy Week?"

"I can't wait," I gushed. Crazy Week is an

Allington Academy tradition. The last week before summer vacation, the school hosts all kinds of fun activities — like Field Day, for example, and Senior Serenade. We still had to go to some classes and stuff, but we finished our final exams last Friday. During Crazy Week nobody really takes the lessons seriously — not even the teachers.

Scott glanced over toward the kitchen, where a slim man in a gray suit was frowning in our direction. "I see my manager over there giving me the evil eye. Better move on to the next table. See you around."

"See you," I called as Scott walked calmly away from us, holding out the silver pitcher of iced tea.

"And speaking of the evil eye," Jenelle added as she looked past Scott. Fiona Von Steig was seated three tables away, stabbing the piece of cake in front of her with her fork. She looked like a deranged cake murderer.

My heart sank a little at the sight of Fiona. "Why is she here?"

"I guess her parents made her come," Jenelle said. "They were all invited months ago — before . . . everything . . ." Jenelle's voice trailed off. She and Fiona used to be best friends. Then they had a fight. Fiona and I used to be friends, too. Well, almost. We were getting there. But then we had a fight, too.

That's kind of the way things go with Fiona.

I sighed. "I still feel bad," I admitted.

"Because you blamed Fiona for something Lucia did?" Jenelle asked. "It was an honest mistake. Fiona had tricked you lots of times before."

"Still, I shouldn't have said all of those things about how she doesn't even know what real friends are." I winced at the memory. I'd been pretty harsh.

"Well . . ." Jenelle toyed with the rim of her water glass. "I guess you could always apologize. If you wanted."

"I've tried."

Jenelle shrugged. "You could try again." She gave me a knowing look, and I sighed again. I knew what she was saying — a few weeks had passed. Maybe Fiona was over it.

I hesitated. "Are *you* going to apologize?"

"That's different — Fiona really *did* trick me," Jenelle shot back. Her hand trembled a bit, and I could tell she was still angry about the way that Fiona had tried to get Jenelle to break up with her crush, Anderson. "She's the one who should apologize."

Just then, Fiona stood up and moved toward

the punch table. My heart started pounding then, the way it does when I'm about to do something scary. It's like my body knows what I'm going to do before my brain does. In a flash, I found myself on my feet. I started after her before I had a chance to really think about it.

"What are you doing?" Jenelle whispered.

"I'm going to try one more time," I told her. I didn't know how Fiona would react. But if I apologized, at least I wouldn't have to feel like I was having a heart attack every time I saw her.

"Fiona," I said, and she turned to face me.

Her blue eyes narrowed when she saw me. "Oh, look who it is." Her voice was colder than the ice cubes floating in the punch. "Amy Flowers. Are you going to accuse me of stealing a cupcake?" She gestured toward the groom's cake display.

I suddenly regretted coming over. But I wasn't going to give up that easily. "No, I — I just wanted to say that I'm sorry. I'm sorry that I mistrusted you. And I'm sorry . . . for what I said."

Fiona's face softened. "Really?" she asked.

"Really," I said warmly. "I mean, we were really becoming friends." I thought about how I'd spent the night at her house, and the quiet time we'd shared in her kitchen as the sun came up. Fiona could be difficult. But she could be sweet, too.

"Wow, Amy, that means so much to me." Fiona blinked a little as if she was fighting tears, although I didn't see any. She reached out and pressed my hand. "Thank you."

"Y-you're welcome," I stammered. *Wow.* I don't know what I'd been expecting . . . but this sure was a shock. My head felt light. *I did the right thing,* I thought. *Fiona forgives me.* Maybe we wouldn't be friends. But we didn't have to be enemies, either. "Well, I — I guess I'm going to head back to my table."

"I'm *so* glad we talked," Fiona said.

"Me too." I smiled at her. Impulsively, I reached out and gave her a quick hug.

Fiona patted my back awkwardly. "Oh, and Amy?" She smiled at me.

"Yes?"

"Have a cupcake," she said. In one lightning move, she plucked one of the small supports holding up the bottom tier of the display. She jumped back as three hundred chocolate cupcakes toppled — all over me. The silver platters clanged and clattered to the floor, and bits of cake and gobs of icing flew everywhere. The band stopped playing and everyone turned to look. Fiona had somehow managed to disappear.

"Oh, my goodness!" It was my mother's voice.

9

Someone raced over. It was Kirk, snapping photos. "Stop that before I murder you," I growled at him as I wiped frosting from my face.

"Death by chocolate!" he crowed, clicking away.

I lunged toward him and slipped in the frosting. "Whoa!" I cried as I fell. Luckily, my fall was cushioned by a few cupcakes. If you call that lucky.

A hand appeared before me, and I grabbed it. "Amy, are you okay?"

It was Scott. *Why does he always show up when something humiliating is happening?* I wondered. I only saw his face for a moment — then everything was blurry. I was fighting tears. But I could see well enough to notice that Fiona was nowhere to be seen.

I felt someone grab my upper arm. "I've got it from here," Jenelle said quickly.

My mom had rushed to the rescue. "I'll help you get cleaned up."

"Actually, Mrs. Flowers, if you'd let the caterer know about the mess, that would be even better," Jenelle said quickly. "I can help Amy in the ladies' room." Her voice was so businesslike that Mom didn't even question it. She just hurried off to organize the cleanup. Jenelle nodded at her mother, who got the band to start up again as we hurried away.

"That's what I get for talking to Fiona," I wailed as Jenelle steered me out of the elegant hall. "I should have known."

"Well, look on the bright side," she replied. "At least you don't owe her an apology anymore."

"There you go," Jenelle said as she snipped a tag from the waistband of my pants. "Good as new. Hey, if you're going to have a cupcake disaster, it pays to have it at my mom's wedding."

I glanced at myself in the gold-edged mirror over the marble sink. We were in the elegant hotel ladies' room, and Jenelle was helping me get changed. My cupcake-covered blue silk dress was slung over the door to a bathroom stall. I was now wearing a champagne silk top over black velvet pants. The clothes were slightly big and a little warm for June in Houston, but beggars can't be choosers. I was just glad not to be sporting the smeared-cupcake look anymore. "Does your mom always drive around with extra clothes in the trunk of her car?"

Jenelle shrugged. "Usually," she admitted. "These are samples for next season." Linda owns Bounce, one of the trendiest boutiques in Houston.

"I'll try not to spill anything on them," I promised.

Jenelle's eyes twinkled. "Lucky for you, there aren't any cupcakes left."

I felt my face burn, and I saw in the mirror that my cheeks were doing their usual red-dot-in-the-center target-style blush thing. "I can't believe I ruined the groom's cake."

"*Fiona* ruined it," Jenelle corrected. "And it really doesn't matter. Mom has little silver frames to give out as party favors, too, so people won't leave empty-handed. Come on." She tugged at my sleeve. "Let's get back to the party."

We trooped out of the ladies' room and into the hallway, which was lined with gilt mirrors and enormous flower arrangements. I could hear the band playing faintly through the double doors. Suddenly, a wave of loud music washed over me as the door opened and my brother walked out.

"I'm *hungry*," he wailed dramatically. "What happened to all of the cupcakes?"

"Do you practice being annoying?" I shot back. "Or does it come naturally?"

Laughing, he shook his shaggy brown hair out of his eyes. "You're just such an easy target."

"Jenelle, darling!" cooed a voice, and a woman with a pouf of gray hair swept over and wrapped an arm around my friend. "Sweetie, your mother is looking for you."

"Okay, Aunt Eileen," Jenelle said. "I'll be right there." She turned to me. "You coming?"

We all stepped inside, and Jenelle hurried across the room with her aunt. The guests were still crowding the dance floor, and the caterers had cleaned up the cupcake disaster. It looked like nothing had happened.

"I can't believe you ruined Uncle Steve's cake," Kirk said as Jenelle and her aunt disappeared into the crowd. "He was *crying* about it."

A wave of panic ran over me. "He *was*?" I felt horrible.

Kirk shook his head. "You really *are* an easy target. Do you seriously think Uncle Steve cares about a bunch of cupcakes? He even picked one up off the floor and ate it. He kept insisting it was even tastier than before."

I laughed weakly. Uncle Steve is basically the sweetest guy on earth. He was already back on the dance floor, grooving with my mom.

"You know, you're still a little crusty," Kirk said, touching my jaw.

"I am?" Sure enough, there was a smear of icing there. I rubbed at it.

"Gone," Kirk said.

"Thanks." I felt myself blush again, and I sneaked a glance toward a nearby table, where

Scott was refilling water glasses. *Why am I always making a fool of myself in front of Scott?* I wondered. My stomach sank, and I felt a little queasy.

"What's wrong?" Kirk asked.

"Nothing," I lied.

"Really? Because you look like you just swallowed a slug." Kirk followed my gaze. "Are you feeling like a loser because you fell on the cupcakes in front of that cute waiter guy?"

"No," I said.

"Uh-huh." Kirk folded his arms across his chest and shot me a dubious look. "Is that why your face is about to burst into flames?"

"Okay, I'm a little embarrassed," I admitted. "I know that guy — he goes to my school. We're friends."

"Ohhhh . . ." Kirk waggled his eyebrows. *"Friends."*

"No, really," I insisted.

"Mmm-hmm." Kirk gave me a knowing look.

"I mean it," I said, but my voice didn't sound convincing, even to me. The fact was, I had no idea *what* we were. Sometimes I thought that Scott like-liked me, but other times, I wasn't so sure.

"Oh, you *mean* it," Kirk nodded, then rolled his eyes. "I get it."

I sighed, and we stood there for a moment

without saying anything. Scott smiled at an elderly gentleman as he refilled his glass. He said something, and the gentleman laughed. "Why don't guys just ask girls out on real dates anymore?" I asked suddenly. "At least then the girl would know if he was interested, or what."

I expected Kirk to shoot back some dumb comment, but instead he seemed to think it over for a minute. "It's not so easy," he said at last. "I mean, what if the girl says no?"

"If he never asks, she can never say *yes*, either," I pointed out. "Instead, everyone just ends up 'hanging out,' not knowing how the other person feels and trying to guess and feeling like an idiot all the time."

Kirk looked at me. "You're right."

"I am?" *Whoa.* I wasn't sure I'd ever heard those two words in that order from my brother before. At least not when he was talking to me.

"Which is surprising, coming from someone with a chunk of cupcake stuck to her shoe."

I looked down. Sure enough, I had cupcake smeared on my right heel. I groaned as Kirk snapped a photo.

These cupcakes are the gift that keeps on giving, I thought.

15

CHAPTER TWO

Amy's Future Careers Day Rule:
Try to pick a future career that will actually exist in the future. Jobs like "Princess of Sixteenth-Century England" don't really count.

"That scone looks awesome," I said, eyeing the breakfast treat on my good friend Michiko Ohara's plate. We were sitting at our usual table in the Allington café before school Monday morning. They have delicious maple-pecan scones, tons of different kinds of muffins, juice, and tea.

"No," Mitchie said.

"No, what?" I asked. "No, it doesn't look awesome?"

"No, you can't have half of it." Mitchie grinned and pulled the plate closer to her. "Get your own."

"Come on, I just want a little piece," I insisted.

"That's what you always say," Mitchie shot back. "And then you steal the whole thing!"

"Oh, hey, here comes Kiwi," I said, pointing over Mitchie's shoulder.

"Nice try, Super-Spy," Mitchie said. "But I'm not taking my eyes off of this scone."

I laughed and touched the brim of my fedora. I had on a trench coat, too. It was the first day of Crazy Week at Allington — Future Careers Day — and everyone was dressed up. Some people took it seriously. Mitchie, for example, had on a blazer and navy skirt — she was dressed as a sports reporter. But most kids used the day as a sort of second Halloween. I mean, I'd already seen two dudes dressed as aliens, which didn't really seem like a future career to me.

"Hey, guys," Kiwi said as she bopped over to us. She was wearing a tutu over a pair of jeans.

"Are you a ballerina?" Mitchie asked.

"Kooky fashion designer," Kiwi explained as she slid into the booth beside Mitchie. "Ooh, scone!" She broke off a piece of Mitchie's break-fast and popped it into her mouth. "Yum!"

I laughed, and Mitchie sighed. She broke off another small piece and handed it to me. She was shaking her head, but she was smiling, too. "Friends," she grumbled.

"Hello, Amy," said a smooth voice at my shoulder. I looked over to see Fiona. She was wearing a purple dress with a wide yellow belt, yellow shoes with super-tall heels, and large round glasses with black frames. Fiona doesn't wear glasses, so I guessed these were fake. "Enjoying your cupcake?" she asked. "I see you're eating it instead of wearing it this time."

"It's a scone," Mitchie corrected. "And *you* could be wearing it, if you don't watch out." Of course, I'd told my friends all about the incident at the wedding. I could tell by the look on Mitchie's face that her blood was boiling as hot as mine was. She and Fiona had a history, too. As in, they used to be friends. Until Fiona invited Mitchie for a sleepover one night and cut off Mitchie's waist-length hair while she was asleep.

It happened a long time ago, but I knew Mitchie still hadn't forgiven her.

Personally, I was so mad about the cupcake incident, I couldn't even speak.

Fiona glared at Mitchie. "Stay out of it."

"Why should I?" Mitchie demanded. "Amy's my friend, Fiona. I know you don't have any idea what that word means, but I do."

For a moment, Fiona looked stricken. "I have friends," she said.

18

Mitchie just looked at her. "Right," she said at last.

Just then, Lucia de Leon strode up to our table. She was still Fiona's friend — and the other member of the League. As in, "They're out of your league." If Fiona was the Queen Bee of the School, Lucia was her Assistant Insect. At that moment, she was wearing a red dress with a wide navy belt cinched at her narrow waist and mile-high navy heels. She didn't have on glasses, but her long, bouncy brown hair was tied up in a bun.

"What are you guys supposed to be, anyway?" Kiwi asked.

Fiona rolled her eyes. "I'm editor in chief of *Vogue* magazine," she said as if it was obvious.

"And what are you?" Mitchie asked Lucia. "Her evil twin?"

Lucia rolled her eyes, too. "Of course not?" she said. Everything Lucia says sounds like a question. If the school was ever on fire, she'd probably scream, "Everyone? Like, stop, drop, and roll?" She glared at Mitchie. "I'm, like, editor in chief of *Bazaar*?"

"Original," Mitchie said.

Lucia grinned. "Thanks?"

"Lucia, do you have the invitations?" Fiona

19

snapped. Clearly, she'd had enough of this conversation.

"Um, yeah?" She sounded a little hesitant. "That's why I came over?" Lucia slowly reached into the hobo bag slung over her shoulder and pulled out a stack of pale yellow envelopes. She handed them carefully to Fiona. "There's, um, something — ?"

Fiona cut her off. "Don't get excited," she said as she handed one to each of us. "I have to invite the whole grade."

"Thanks for the warning," Mitchie said as she turned the thick, creamy envelope over in her hands.

"It's for Beach Day," Fiona explained.

"What's that?" I asked. This was my first year at Allington, so I didn't know all of the traditions.

"It's a big party at Fiona's beach house the first Saturday after school ends," Mitchie explained. "It isn't really a school event, but everyone goes, anyway. Fiona's family provides buses, and the school provides chaperones."

"Oh!" Kiwi cried as she scanned the invitation. "Cool, Lucia — it's at *your* house this year!"

Fiona's eyes went wide as if she'd just swallowed something sharp. She snatched the invitation from my fingers. "What?!" she screeched.

She looked over at Lucia, her eyes spouting fire. "You said you'd print up invitations for *my* party!"

For a moment, Lucia looked like she wanted to run and hide. But then she straightened up and gritted her teeth as if she was about to head into battle. "What's the big deal?" Lucia planted a hand on her hip. "I mean, my house is bigger than yours? And my family can cater?" The de Leons owned a chain of popular restaurants in Houston. "And, like, you always throw parties?"

Fiona's jaw dropped. Her mouth opened and closed silently, like a marionette. Wow, a speechless Fiona. That's something you don't see every day.

"Hey, Lucia!" Voe Silk, one of the most popular girls in the eighth grade, waved and smiled. She seemed to be dressed as a gorgeous runway model, but I wasn't sure if that was her future career or just a regular outfit. "Can't wait for Saturday!" Voe called.

"You invited the eighth grade?" Fiona cried.

Lucia smiled. It was a strange little smile — half smug, half scared. Without a word, she turned and walked away. Fiona stood stock-still for a moment. She placed my invitation back on the table. Then she followed Lucia.

"That was weird," Kiwi said. "I think I'm going to get some tea." She got up and headed toward the counter.

"Fiona had better watch her back," Mitchie said as I tucked the invitation into one of the outer pockets of my huge bag.

"I'm more worried about Lucia," I said. "Fiona's going to be on the warpath now."

"We'll see." Mitchie shrugged. "Lucia is way sneakier than she seems."

"Kirk is always saying to watch out for people who act like airheads," I told her. I thought about that for a minute. "Then again, Kirk is always wrong."

"He seems pretty smart to me," Mitchie said. Her eyes were fastened on the table.

"Oh, please," I told her. "You haven't watched him try to clean the kitchen counter with his sock."

Mitchie giggled, which was kind of weird for her. She isn't really a giggler. And her cheeks were pink — also weird. She's not much of a blusher, either. *Does she have a little crush on my brother?* I wondered. Mitchie had never said anything about it to me, but sometimes I thought so. I was never really sure how I felt about it. I guessed it was a little awkward for my friend to have a crush on my brother. Then again, why not? It was just a crush, right?

Mitchie seemed to notice me looking at her, because all of a sudden, her eyes locked with mine. The pink in her cheeks deepened, and she looked away. "What's taking Kiwi so long?" she asked suddenly. "The bell is about to ring."

I looked over at the counter. "Oh, she's talking to Anderson." I waved at my lab partner, Anderson Sempe, but he didn't notice. Kiwi didn't notice, either. They seemed pretty deep in conversation.

"I didn't know those guys were friends," Mitchie said.

"Me neither. I mean, of course they *know* each other." I cocked my head. Mitchie had a point. They were looking pretty intense. A strange shiver ran up the back of my neck, and I wondered why. *What could be wrong with Kiwi talking to Anderson?* I thought. I didn't have an answer. *Okay, sure, he's Jenelle's crush. But that doesn't mean he can't talk to other girls.*

The weird feeling didn't exactly go away, but I didn't feel bad about ignoring it. After all, Anderson wasn't like Lucia or Fiona. He was sweet. You didn't have to worry that he would try to trick you. Thankfully.

23

Goodness knows I had enough people like *that* in my life.

"All right, class, all right, all right, all riiight!" Mr. Pearl's dark eyes bugged out of his head even more than usual as he stared out at the lab tables. He had given us a simple experiment to do, but most of the kids were just chatting with one another and laughing. "This lab counts as part of your class participation grade, so I suggest you all simmer down! Just simmer down! Simmer!" He took a swig from his brushed steel commuter mug. Mr. Pearl drank a lot of coffee, which was probably why he was always so full of energy.

"But we already took the final," Preston Harringford pointed out. "None of the other teachers are making us work in class." Preston was dressed as a punk rocker — he'd even styled his hair into a blue Mohawk.

Mr. Pearl pointed at Preston. "Simmer!" he commanded.

The gong that signaled the end of class — at Allington, the headmistress believes in "gentle, calming tones" — chimed.

"Okay, class dismissed." Mr. Pearl grinned. "Get out of here. Shoo!" He flapped his hands. "Go pester someone else!"

24

Everyone laughed and chatted as they gathered their things. I looked over at Anderson, who was writing something in his notebook. He didn't even seem to have noticed the bell.

"Hey, Amy!" Preston hopped up onto my lab table and grinned cockily. "Just the person I need to see."

"Then get your rear end off my lab table," I told him. "That surface has enough germs."

"Good one." Preston laughed, but he didn't budge. He looked over his shoulder, then leaned in closely. "Seriously, though," he whispered, "it's about the Seventh Grade Prank."

"Forget it."

Preston looked shocked. "But I need your help! Last year's prank was lame."

"Look, I'm not getting into any more of your crazy shenanigans," I told him.

"Shenanigans?" he repeated. "I don't even know what that word means!"

"It means whatever insane thing your brain has cooked up," I snapped. I shoved my notebook into my green-and-blue backpack. "I can't afford another detention." A couple of months ago, Preston and I had worked together on a school-sponsored volunteer project. It had led to major trouble. Which led to a detention in which we had

25

to help out in the kitchen. Which led to a pudding fight. Which almost led to another detention. "It may be Crazy Week, but I'm not that crazy."

"But the school *expects* each grade to pull a prank," Preston insisted. "We won't get into trouble."

I snorted.

"Look, I need the assistance of your evil brain," Preston went on.

"My brain isn't evil."

"Are you kidding? You're even dressed as a super-spy!" Preston pounded the table with his palm. "You have to help. Doesn't she, Anderson?"

"Hmm?" Anderson looked up from his notebook. When he noticed us, he slammed it closed. "What? What are we talking about?"

"Welcome back, earthling — we're talking about . . ." Preston leaned over and whispered dramatically, "The *prank*."

Anderson's blue eyes were wide, and he looked even spacier than usual. This wasn't helped by the fact that he was dressed as a chef, and his floppy white hat had fallen at an awkward angle. "What about the bank?"

Preston groaned, rolling his eyes.

"Hey, y'all," Jenelle said as she walked up to join us. She smiled at Anderson. "Hey."

Anderson quickly tucked his notebook into his messenger bag. "Hey." His cheeks turned bright pink.

"Jenelle, please tell Amy that she has to help me." Preston clasped his hands together as if he was begging.

Obediently, Jenelle turned to me. "Preston needs help," she said.

"Tell me about it," I agreed. "Look, the bell is about to ring," I told Preston. "Can we argue about this later?"

"That means yes!" he crowed.

"Grr!" I grabbed my bag. I gave Jenelle a wave and hurried down the hall. *How can one person be so annoying?* I wondered as I darted down the stairs. I mean, Preston could be cool sometimes. But he could also be a royal pain. *And he never gives up!*

Just as I was about to make it to the ground floor, I felt a tug on my ponytail. I couldn't believe Preston had followed me! I told him I'd talk to him later! "Quit it!" I yelled, turning around.

Scott stopped in his tracks and blinked in surprise. "Sorry," he said.

"Oh! Oh . . . Scott. No — *I'm* sorry. I thought — I thought —" I shook my head. My brain wasn't working properly. Partly because I was

27

surprised . . . and partly because Scott was dressed in a sharp black suit and looked even handsomer than usual. "I thought you were someone else," I said finally.

"No big deal — I shouldn't go around grabbing ponytails, anyway." He smiled, and I wanted to crawl away. "So, hey, I was wondering if you wanted to . . ." Scott chuckled a little and shifted his weight from one foot to another, almost as if he was embarrassed.

Omigosh . . .

A thought swept over me slowly as I watched Scott's eyes dart away shyly.

Is it . . . could he be . . . is he asking me out?

The words I'd said to Kirk two days ago echoed in my mind: *Why don't guys just ask girls out on real dates anymore? At least then the girl would know if he was interested, or what.*

I wished it would happen, and now it's happening. . . .

Scott ran a hand through his floppy sandy-blond hair. "I was wondering if you wanted to join my team for the balloon relay on Field Day. We need an extra person."

And — *splat.* That's the noise my hopes made as they fell off a cliff. "Oh," I said brightly, trying to cover my disappointment. "Sure."

"It'll be fun."

"Right." I forced myself to smile at him. "Sounds great."

"And maybe we can hang out afterward."

"Okay." I nodded. "Well, I've . . . uh —" I gestured over my shoulder.

"Right, I'm late, too. See you tomorrow, Spygirl!" He winked and walked away.

I sighed, fighting the disappointment in my chest. Okay, so I'd told Kirk that I wished things were clear. *Does Scott want to be my boyfriend, or my friend boy? Well, things were getting more crystal by the moment. Balloon race plus hanging out with the team equals friend boy.*

I'm glad I know, I thought as I turned and headed down the hall. *I'm glad.*

I'm really glad.

I think.

CHAPTER THREE

Amy's Field
Day Rule: Try to avoid any games involving mud, shaving cream, squirt guns, Silly String, tossing eggs, water balloons, and/or eating massive amounts of Jell-O with your hands tied behind your back. Or, you know, just bring a change of clothes.

"Okay, I've seen what we're up against, and I think we've got this nailed," Preston said the next day. He rubbed his hands excitedly. "We've got the speed, we've got the talent — we've just got to go for it. Come on, let's win this! Team cheer!"

Mitchie stared at him from beneath her black bangs. "Preston, it's just a relay race."

"Look, I'm not taking home another honorable mention!" Preston insisted, holding up a fistful of yellow ribbons. "I want a blue! Who's with me?"

"We're all with you," I told him. "You're the one who made us be on your team, remember?" I looked out across the lush green field, which was crowded with students. We were using part of the Allington golf course for our Field Day relays. At the far end, a group had just taken off on a sack race. Another group was working on Super Soaker tag. I spotted Scott halfway across the field. He was searching frantically through a pile of shoes to find his own, then race back to his team. I wondered if he remembered that he'd asked me to be on his balloon relay team. According to the schedule, it was coming up in about fifteen minutes.

"Okay, line up, line up," Preston insisted. He held a plastic pitcher and a bunch of red plastic cups. "Anderson, help me here."

Anderson started handing out full cups of water to everyone on our team.

"What are we doing again?" Jenelle asked as she took the cup from Anderson's fingers.

"You take the water and run to that pickle jar." Preston pointed to a large jar about fifty yards away. "Dump in your water, then run back. The first team to fill the jar wins."

"So you don't want to spill any," Mitchie said.

Kiwi nodded. "But you still want to move fast."

31

"I'm telling you, we have this nailed," Preston said. "None of the other teams want that blue ribbon the way we do. They don't have that *hunger*. Eye of the tiger!" He punched his fist in the air.

Mitchie cocked an eyebrow. "I seriously hope you're kidding right now."

"I am." Preston shrugged. "Kind of."

Still, I found myself looking around at the other teams. Fiona's group was next to ours. When she saw me looking at her, she narrowed her eyes and turned away.

I was actually kind of surprised to see that she had agreed to take part in any of the games. It didn't seem like her style. Then again, she'd managed to participate without getting a single speck of dirt on her navy eyelet halter top or white shorts. Pretty impressive.

"Okay, line up," Mitchie announced. "We're about to start."

We took our places. The whistle blew, and Preston took off with a weird low-to-the-ground lope. He reached the pickle jar fast and without spilling a drop. Then he raced back and tagged Jenelle. She has a really smooth walk, so she didn't spill anything. But she wasn't that fast, either. Mitchie was fast, but she spilled some of her water. Surprisingly, Kiwi managed to jog in her usual bouncy way — and not spill anything. I couldn't figure out how that was possible. Our jar was almost three-quarters full when Anderson took off. But he hadn't gone three steps before he tripped.

"Whoa!" he shouted as water sloshed over the rim of his cup. He windmilled his right arm and tottered forward. He reached the jar and dumped in his water — less than a third of his glass.

"You have to give this all you got," Preston said, clapping me on the back. "You're the anchor that holds this team together — this is our last chance at gold!"

"If we win, can I be the one on the front of the cereal box?" I joked.

"Who else?" Preston demanded. "You can be the sneaker spokesperson, too! But I'm taking the car endorsements."

Anderson touched my hand and I trotted forward. But the water in my cup lapped at the edge. I slowed way down, but that was worse. In the end, I felt myself crouching low to the ground and thrusting my legs way out in front. *I'm doing Preston's crazy walk*, I realized. But it worked, so I went with it.

By the time I reached the pickle jar, I still

had most of my water. I dumped it in — we were almost to the top! Then I turned and ran like crazy.

"Come on, Amy!" Mitchie shouted.

"You can do it!" Kiwi cried.

"Eye of the tiger!" Preston was all googly-eyed — he looked completely crazy.

I saw Fiona heading toward me. She was taking little mincing steps and scowling at her cup. I was just about to pass her when I felt my front foot slip. I stuck out my arm to regain my balance, but I pitched face-first into the grass. "Oof!"

I felt a foot on my arm, then heard a screech as Fiona tripped beside me. Water had sloshed all over her. She spluttered angrily, like a leaky faucet. "What have you *done*?" she screeched.

"Sorry," I said as my friends raced over to help me up.

"Amy, are you okay?" Kiwi held out a hand and pulled me to my feet.

"I'm fine," I said, dusting off my legs.

"Nice try, taking out the competition," Preston teased. "Only next time, try not to blow it for our team."

"I didn't do it on purpose!" I insisted, casting a glance at Fiona. She was still glowering. "I really didn't."

"She slipped in the water I spilled," Anderson said guiltily.

"What-ever, she deserves it," Mitchie growled. "It's cupcake payback." She and Fiona had a momentary Glare Off, and I felt a little awkward. After all, Fiona *did* sort of deserve a little slosh. Then again, it really *was* an accident.

I mean, if I'm going to get back at someone, it should really be on purpose.

"Now I have to get this top dry-cleaned!" Fiona snarled.

"Sorry, Fiona," Anderson said. Poor guy. He clearly did feel bad about the minor spill.

"Big deal, send your mom's assistant to do it," Mitchie shot back. "It's not like it's a problem for *you*."

Fiona ignored her. "Thanks a lot, Amy."

"I honestly didn't do it on purpose," I said again. But I was starting to lose my patience. *What's the big deal, anyway? It's just a little water.*

"Sorry, Fiona," Anderson chimed in again.

Jenelle patted Anderson on the shoulder encouragingly, but Preston just rolled his eyes. "Sure, Amy. Whatever you say. Just be sure to look that innocent when we pull the prank."

"What?" Fiona screeched. *"You* aren't pulling

any pranks. I'm organizing the prank, Preston Harringford. Of course."

"No way!" Preston folded his arms across his chest. "Amy and I are in charge this year."

"Whoa, whoa, whoa —" I said as Fiona set her blue-laser eyes on me. "I never agreed to —"

"Hey, Amy." Scott had suddenly appeared at my elbow, smiling in his heart-melting way. "It's time for the balloon race." He was holding a tray full of balloons filled with shaving cream. "You're still on my team, right?"

But before I could say yes, Fiona grabbed a balloon and nailed me with it. Shaving cream exploded all over.

Fiona smiled smugly. "Now we're even."

"Even?" I was furious. Before I had time to think, I reached for a balloon. I chucked it as hard as I could, but Fiona ducked . . . and I nailed Preston in the side of the head.

"Um, we kind of need to save these for the race —" Scott started. But he had both hands on the tray, so there wasn't much he could do.

"Who did that?" Preston asked. Fiona pointed at me. *"Amy?"*

"No — wait!"

Laughing, Preston grabbed a balloon. Three seconds later, I was covered in shaving cream.

"Wow." Scott's eyes were huge as he looked at me from head to toe. "Did you bring some clothes to change into or something? You know — for when we hang out later?"

I shook my head. "No, but — I mean, I'm sure the whole team will be covered in shaving cream. Right?"

"Whole team?" Scott asked. He looked blank.

"The whole team is hanging out after Field Day," I said. My tongue felt heavy and my head felt light as I gazed into his deep-brown eyes. I could tell by the look on his face that he had no idea what I was talking about.

"I thought it would just be you and me," Scott said. "I mean, if that's okay. . . ."

I looked down at my outfit. *Okay?* I was covered in grass stains and shaving goop. My hair was hanging down in limp snakes. I looked like a visitor from Planet Gross.

Kiwi was waggling her eyebrows at me, as if I was headed off for True Romance. *Pardon me while I strangle my friend*, I thought as I smiled weakly at Scott. But what could I do? What could I say?

I gulped.

"Sure," I said at last. "Sounds great."

*   *   *

"Want to trade?" Scott asked, holding out his bag of candy.

"Hmm . . . depends." I crunched down on my chocolate-raspberry malted milk ball. We'd just been to Sugar's Candy Shack, which has the best selection of candies in Houston. Scott and I each had a plastic sack filled with a mix of different sweets. "What've you got?"

"I'll trade you two Swedish Fish for a chocolate shark."

I snorted. "You have *got* to be kidding."

Scott laughed. "Okay, a sour gummy worm and three chocolate-covered raisins."

"Raisins . . ." I pretended to think it over. "Those are practically health food. Make it a worm and a toffee frog."

"Deal," Scott said, and I handed over the shark.

"You're a tough negotiator." Scott grinned as I bit the head off of the worm. Or maybe it was the tail. I'm not sure. All I know is that it tasted like a really sour lime.

"You still have your raisins," I pointed out.

"Oh, jeez, look who's here," said a loud voice behind me. A moment later, Kirk ran up and leaped in front of me. "Ooh, candy!" He reached for my bag, and I tossed it to Scott.

"Sorry, man," Scott said. "I'm protecting this."

"Better not let the Creature from the Slime Lagoon get it," Kirk said, looking at me.

"Ha-ha." I touched my hair self-consciously. I had tried to rinse it out in the girls' room sink, but it was sticky. Yuck.

"What happened to you?" Kirk asked. "You look like you just won a Nickelodeon Kids' Choice Award. Like you went up to get your statue and a big vat of goop just splattered all over your head —"

"I get it," I told him.

"I think Amy looks like she's been having fun," Scott said. It was sweet of him, but I couldn't help feeling like he sounded a little like my dad when he said it.

"What are you doing here, anyway?" I asked Kirk. We were standing in the Rice Village, a section of Houston that's crowded with fashionable stores and cafés. And it's not like Kirk is into shopping. Or coffee.

"I'm meeting Alizae," Kirk said. He gave me a huge smile. "And here she is."

"Hi!" Alizae has long, black hair and beautiful dark eyes. For a while, I suspected that she might be Kirk's girlfriend. But it turned out that she's his math tutor. Now, her slim eyebrows arched. For a moment, she looked stumped. I was wondering if she'd forgotten my name when she asked, "Amy, do you want to borrow my comb?"

Do I really look that bad? I wondered. A flash of panic shivered through me, but it passed quickly. *Chill out*, I told myself. *It doesn't really matter if you look like a supermodel or a squid. It's not like Scott and I are on a date, or anything. We're just hanging out.* "I'm good," I told Alizae.

"I just realized that we need to go to Sugar's Candy Shack immediately," Kirk informed Alizae. "I'm buying."

Alizae grinned. "Sounds great. See you guys later?" She waved, and she and my brother walked off down the street. I sighed. Alizae's long hair gleamed in the sun and she wore a clean white T-shirt over a dark denim mini. She was the kind of person who always looked great — without trying. I wondered what that would be like.

"Hey, look," Scott said, pointing to a nearby restaurant.

I looked over and caught sight of a girl who looked like she'd just been slimed. Half of her hair was plastered to her head and the other half was jutting out like a tumbleweed. Her clothes were dirty and stained. I was just about to say, "Yeah, she needs some serious help," when I realized that I was looking at my own reflection in a plate-glass window. Scott was actually pointing to the people eating at a table in front of the glass.

Wow, I thought. *I really* do *look that bad.*

"Isn't that your friend?" Scott asked.

He was right, of course. It was Anderson. He was sitting at an outdoor café table, and a girl with waist-length auburn hair was with him — her back was to me. *It's Kiwi*, I realized after a moment. They were leaning closely together, and it looked as if they were whispering.

"We're just running into everyone," Scott said brightly. "Want to go say hi?"

I hesitated. Something about how they were sitting — so closely — told me that they didn't want to be interrupted. "Maybe not."

Scott raised an eyebrow, but he just nodded. "Okay."

We walked around a little more, swapping candy and chatting. After a while, I completely forgot that I looked horrible. I was glad we were hanging out and that we were just friends. It was easy — and it was way less awkward than it had been in the past. Usually, whenever I'm with Scott, I'm wondering how he feels about me or if he thinks we're on a date or how he can be so handsome. But this time, I could just talk to him. It was *comfortable*.

After a while, we ended up in front of my house. We paused at the end of the walk, and Scott smiled. "So," he said.

"So," I repeated.

"This was fun," Scott said. "We should do it again."

"Oh, yeah!" I agreed warmly. "Definitely."

"We could even see a movie sometime. Maybe get dinner," Scott went on.

"Sure," I replied. I was about to make a joke about how dinner and a movie would seem like a date when Scott leaned over and kissed me on the cheek. Then he turned and walked away.

The whole thing happened so quickly that I wondered if I'd dreamed it.

But there was my cheek, warm and still slightly damp from the kiss. I reached up and touched the place where his lips had been.

Wait a minute . . . what just happened? Was that — were we just on a date*?*

It actually seemed like we were!

My head was spinning. *So much for clarity.*

CHAPTER FOUR

Amy's Date
Rule #1:
Try to figure out if it's actually a date. Then worry about the other rules.

"So — wait — he kissed you?" Mitchie's voice was practically a squeal as she patted a sticky popcorn ball into shape.

"Kind of," I admitted. It was later the same night, and Mitchie and I were discussing the maybe-kind-of-date I'd just had. My brain was still churning like a crazed hamster on a wheel, trying to make sense of the whole thing. "It was just on the cheek, and it was really fast. So maybe it was just a friendship kiss."

Mitchie looked doubtful. "A friendship kiss?" she asked. "Is Scott from France?"

"No," I admitted.

"American guys don't give out friendship kisses." She set the popcorn ball neatly on the tray next to six of its brothers. We were making them to share with our friends on Thursday, for the Love Feast. Everyone brings one of their favorite foods to their homeroom for the feast. The only rule is, you can't eat your own — and you can't feed yourself. Someone else has to feed you one of their favorites. Usually, you don't get to bring snacks into the classrooms, but during Crazy Week, anything goes. "If he wanted to be your friend," Mitchie went on, "he would have punched you in the arm."

"I guess."

Just then, the phone rang. Someone picked it up before I had a chance to rinse my hands and wipe them on a kitchen towel. Mitchie picked a dried cherry out of the bowl. "I'm so glad you said we should add these."

"Hey, doofus," Kirk said as he strolled into the kitchen. He held out the phone. "It's for you."

I made a face at him and grabbed the phone as he headed over to the popcorn balls.

"Can I have one?" Kirk asked Mitchie. "They look delicious."

"Why so polite?" I gave Kirk a look as Mitchie handed him the largest popcorn ball.

"Because Mitchie is actually nice," Kirk replied.

Mitchie smiled shyly as I held the phone up to my ear. "Hello?"

"Hey, Amy — it's Scott."

"Oh, hi," I said. I guess Mitchie noticed the surprise in my voice, because she looked up at me. *Scott*, I mouthed, pointing at the phone.

She pursed her lips in a knowing way.

"Listen, I really had a great time today."

"Yeah, me too." I balanced myself uncomfortably on the edge of the stool that Mom keeps in the corner. For some reason, I really didn't want to be having this conversation.

"Well, on my way home, I noticed that *Football Rock Star* is playing at the multiplex. Do you want to go see it on Thursday?"

Football Rock Star was a new musical comedy about a total jock who joins a band to impress a girl. According to just about everyone, it was totally hilarious. I'd been dying to see it. So why did I hesitate before saying okay?

Not that Scott noticed. "Great! There's a four o'clock show, so you can just meet me at the park before, all right?"

"Sure," I said. "Sounds good." There was a weird little beat of silence, and then I said, "So, listen, I'm kind of in the middle of something."

"No problem. See you at school!"

"See you," I said. Then I hung up.

Mitchie eyed my face carefully. "That doesn't look like joy and excitement. What happened?"

"What did your boyfriend want?" Kirk asked as he attacked another popcorn ball.

"He's not my boyfriend," I said automatically. "I think," I added. "Anyway, he just wants to go to the movies on Thursday."

"Hmm," Mitchie said.

"A movie is a date," Kirk announced.

"Maybe," I admitted. Still, Scott and I had been on kind-of-dates before. And they'd always turned out to be kind-of-*not*-dates. "It's weird — I was just getting used to the idea that we're just friends."

"I thought you wanted clarity," Kirk said, leaning against the kitchen island. "I thought you wished boys would just ask girls out on real dates. Now you have one, and you don't want it?"

"No, I do," I insisted. "I think. Maybe I was wrong about that."

"No, you were right!" Kirk was grinning.

Mitchie caught his smile and blushed. "What do you mean?" she asked in a shy voice.

"I mean that I finally got some clarity myself! Amy told me that guys needed to be clear if they liked a girl." He turned to me. "So I took your advice, Amy — I asked Alizae out on a date!" Then he punched Mitchie on the arm. "And she said *yes* — can you believe it?"

For a moment, the kitchen was so silent that I heard water drip from the faucet into the sink. *Drip, drip, drip . . .*

Mitchie was looking down at the place on her arm where Kirk had just punched her. Then she looked up at me. Her eyes were glistening — as if tears might spill over the edges at any moment.

No! I wanted to shout. *I didn't tell Kirk to ask out Alizae! That's not what I said!* But I didn't dare say that. Mitchie would be humiliated.

Luckily, Kirk didn't seem to notice that we were frozen in place. "Man," he said, reaching for another popcorn ball. "These are *awesome!*"

"Um, listen, I've got to get going," Mitchie said quickly. Her short black hair fell across her face as she fumbled with her apron. By the time she looked up, her tears were gone. "I've got a ton of homework."

"I thought Amy said it was Crazy Week," Kirk said.

"Not homework," Mitchie corrected herself. "I meant housework. I told my mom I'd help her out."

47

Kirk rolled his eyes. "You're too nice," he said.

"Yeah." Mitchie cleared her throat. "Well, I guess I'll see you tomorrow," she said to me.

"Don't you want to stay a little longer?" I asked. I was hoping that maybe Kirk would leave and we could talk or something.

"I really can't," Mitchie said. She pressed her lips together, then pointed to the popcorn balls. "You'll bring these Thursday, right?"

"If Kirk can stop eating them," I joked.

But Mitchie only managed a small smile before she ducked out the back door.

Kirk watched the door slam shut behind her. "She's really sweet," he said.

I wanted to shake him. *Why are guys so dumb sometimes?*

CHAPTER FIVE

Amy's Senior Serenade Day Rule: Try not to get involved.

"All right, people — simmer down! I want to see simmering!" Mr. Pearl cupped his hands around his mouth so that he could be heard over all of the chatter. It was Wednesday, and the entire seventh grade was packed into Allington's Blue Parlor. Students were everywhere — sitting on the floor, draped across dark wood furniture, propped up against pristine powder-blue walls. We were supposed to be composing our song for the Senior Serenade. Every class from the sixth to eleventh grade was supposed to sing a farewell to the seniors at a special assembly later that day. "Everyone!" Mr. Pearl's eyes bugged. "We need to get started here, or we'll be singing 'Row, Row, Row Your Boat' in front of the whole school!"

"I already gave you a great idea!" Emmett Daly shouted.

"I don't see how you riding a motorcycle through a flaming hoop is possible, legal, or desirable," Mr. Pearl replied. "It's not even musical!"

"I've got a kazoo." That was from Don Trebuchet, Emmett's best friend. "I could play along."

Mr. Pearl took a deep pull from his commuter mug of coffee. He sipped it the way most people would take a deep breath. He swallowed, then gave his head a little shake. "Next idea," he announced.

There was a small cough from the rear corner. Fiona's manicured fingers hung limply in the air.

"Yes, Fiona?" Mr. Pearl said. "Do you have something sane to add to this discourse?"

"Well, the seniors always really like it when people make a big deal about the fact that they're leaving." Fiona studied her cuticles as if she wasn't really that interested in what she had to say. "I was thinking we could do a song about how much we'll miss them and put it to the tune of 'I Hope You Dance.'"

50

Lucia gasped. "I love that song?" Excited murmurs ran around the room, and Fiona smiled smugly.

Someone at the front of the room made a retching noise.

"Mr. Harringford." Mr. Pearl frowned at Preston, who had just scrambled to his feet. "You'd better have something helpful to say. If it involves motorcycles or flames, I'm sending you directly to Mr. Denton." Mr. Denton was the dean of students — or, as I like to think of him, the Guy Who Gives People Detention.

"No motorcycles," Preston promised. He turned to speak to the rest of the room. "Look, everyone knows that the seniors like funny songs. I was thinking we could sing to the tune of that song that goes, you know, 'We will, we will rock you.' Only we could sing, 'We will, we will *mock* you!' Then we could make fun of the seniors."

"Like what?" Kiwi asked.

"Like how they always hang out on Senior Corner," Preston said. "And how they think they're so great now, but they're about to be freshmen in college — back at the bottom of the heap."

"We could sing about Officer Chang," Mitchie suggested, and everyone laughed. Owen Chang was a senior hall monitor who took his job *way* too seriously.

"And Twenty-eight!" someone else called out.

Twenty-eight was a guy who once ate twenty-eight of the cafeteria's chocolate chip cookies in a row on a dare. He was a school legend.

"Perfect!" Preston cried. "Besides, that song is excellent, because we'll get to stomp and clap."

Fiona snorted. "Look, Preston, that's a cute idea and everything." She squinched up her face on the word "cute," as if the idea made her ill. "But I think the seniors want to feel the love."

"Mockery *is* love," Preston insisted.

The room exploded with excited chatter. On one side of the room, a group of girls burst into a quavery soprano version of "I Hope You Dance." Emmett and Don retaliated by stomping and clapping.

"People, people, people, control yourselves!" Mr. Pearl cried. "I want to see simmering, or you'll all be singing 'Jailhouse Rock' with Mr. Denton!"

Everyone quieted down, and I raised my hand. "Maybe we should vote on it," I suggested.

"Thank you, Amy, for talking some sense." Mr. Pearl flashed me a grateful smile. "People, we're having a vote! Everyone take out a piece of scrap paper and write down the name of the song you want: 'I Hope You Dance' or 'We Will Rock You.'"

"'Mock You,'" Preston corrected.

"'Mock You.'" Mr. Pearl nodded. "Right. And I want to see simmering, people! Simmering mockery!"

There was some quiet commotion as people ripped pages from notebooks and borrowed pens from one another. After a few moments, everyone handed their votes to the front of the room. Mr. Pearl made two piles on the elegant dark wood table beside the fireplace. At first, it looked as if "I Hope You Dance" would win. But then the votes started piling up for "We Will Mock You." After a while, the vote was split — fifty-six for one, and fifty-six for the other. And there were only two votes left. . . .

Mr. Pearl held up the scrap of paper. "Flaming motorcycle kazoo symphony," he read aloud. "Who wrote this?" He glared down at Emmett.

"It's a write-in vote!" Emmett protested.

"And it loses," Mr. Pearl said, dumping the paper into the wastebasket.

"One vote left," Preston pointed out to nobody in particular. His voice sounded breathless.

I sneaked a glance over at Fiona. She was staring at her cuticles again, but I could tell that she was gnawing on the inside of her cheek. I didn't know if she cared about the song — but I knew how much she hated to lose.

Mr. Pearl opened the paper and gave a small chuckle. "We Will Mock You," he read.

The room exploded into cheers and groans. Preston grinned as Don clapped him on the back.

"Thank you, Amy, for helping us come to a decision," Mr. Pearl said. "All right, everyone, let's get to work. We have some lyrics to write!"

"How about — 'He had cookies on a plate! Twenty-eight! He ate more than anyone in the state!'" Preston suggested.

The class laughed, and Mr. Pearl typed the lyrics into the keyboard. His screen was projected onto the wall behind him. The students started buzzing with ideas.

I sneaked another glance over at Fiona. She glared at me and shook her head. I knew what she was thinking — *one vote*. She'd lost by one vote.

My vote.

I sighed. It seemed like no matter what I did, I always ended up directly in Fiona's line of fire.

"What's going on?" I asked Jenelle as we trooped outside to the front courtyard. Lights were flashing throughout the hallways as a firm, polite woman's voice announced, "Fire. Fire. Fire. Please move calmly to the exits. Fire. Fire. Fire. Please move calmly to the exits."

"I guess it's just a drill," Jenelle said. "The teachers don't seem worried about it."

This was true. Ms. Glock was standing at the end of the hallway with Mr. Rivers. Both were laughing as students filed past them.

"Someone probably just pulled an alarm." Jenelle shrugged. "It happens during Crazy Week sometimes."

"Like a prank?" I asked. I knew that class pranks — like the one Preston wanted me to help plan — were usually pulled on Friday, the last day of Crazy Week. "That seems kind of lame. Especially since we were just writing song lyrics — not even in class or anything."

"It is lame," Jenelle agreed. "But it's easy, and if people can't think of anything better, sometimes they get desperate."

The courtyard was crowded with students and teachers trying to herd them into their proper "fire drill head count locations." All the teachers had an electronic notepad with the day's official attendance report for the group they were overseeing at that moment. The teachers were supposed to check off every name to make sure that we'd all left the building safely.

Mr. Pearl ticked off names with a stylus. "Amy Flowers, got you," he said as he touched the screen. "Jenelle Renwick, got you."

Once the teachers finished taking attendance, students started milling around. "Where did Mitchie go?" I asked, a moment before I heard a familiar *thunk*, *scraaaaape*.

Mitchie was on the steps, practicing her grinds. She must have disappeared so that she could grab her skateboard from her locker before dashing to the courtyard. Typical. That girl never lost an opportunity to practice skateboarding.

She rolled up to a step and slid across it with the wood of her board. But at the last moment, she wiped out. The board skidded away as she landed on her rear end.

"Ms. Ohara." Mr. Denton appeared from nowhere, a blue slip in his hand. "I'll see you after school."

"Detention?" Mitchie cried. She clambered to her feet. "But it's Crazy Week!"

"Not all of us have gone crazy, Ms. Ohara," Mr. Denton replied calmly. He took out a handkerchief and wiped his bald head, which was starting to gleam in the hot sun. He held out the blue slip, and Mitchie had no choice but to take it.

"I saw that, Mr. Daly!" Mr. Denton shouted a nanosecond after Emmett splashed some water from the fountain at Don. He turned stiffly and strode away with his purposeful take-no-prisoners walk, shouting, "You and your cohorts can give me ten laps around the lacrosse field!"

"Hey," Jenelle said gently as we walked over to join our friend. "That's annoying." She waved at the blue slip.

Mitchie just shrugged. "Eh, I'll get to spend some quality time with Gerardo." Gerardo was the very sweet, cheerful groundskeeper. Mitchie got detentions for her skateboarding on a fairly regular basis, and she and Gerardo had become pretty friendly. "Besides, I like gardening." She smiled at me quickly. Then she seemed to think of something and looked away.

"Hey, has anyone seen Anderson?" Jenelle asked. She stood on tiptoe to peer through the crowd of students. The entire middle school was in the front courtyard, and everyone had started to mill around. I'm sure it was even crazier behind the library, where the elementary school was gathered. "I've got to tell him something."

"I think I saw him over near the fountain," Mitchie volunteered.

"Be right back," Jenelle said quickly.

Mitchie had been a little quiet with me all morning. It was almost like she was avoiding me. Not like she was angry . . . more like she felt weird. After the Kirk stuff, I didn't blame her.

"So, hey," I said after a minute. "I just wanted to let you know, um . . ." I cleared my throat, unsure how to continue.

Mitchie lifted her eyebrows.

Okay, now I've started, so I just have to finish. I had to push the words out — as awkward as it was. "Well, I just wanted to say that I didn't tell Kirk to ask out Alizae. I never said that. At all."

Mitchie looked at me, pink blooming in her cheeks. "What are you talking about?"

"Just — you know, it wasn't . . . I wouldn't do that to you. I know you kind of . . ."

"What?" Mitchie cried. "Do you think I have a crush on your *brother* or something?" She snorted. "That would be . . ." She shook her head. "That would be weird." Then she laughed this peculiar little laugh that made her sound like someone dangling over a shark tank.

I didn't know what to say. I was having a moment of *Wait — am I completely nuts?*

Mitchie looked worried, like she was afraid I didn't believe her and might call her on it. But I wasn't about to. I felt like enough of an idiot already. I mean, maybe I had just imagined the whole Kirk thing. Or maybe she just didn't want to admit it. Either way, there wasn't much I could say about it.

Lucky for me, Jenelle chose that moment to reappear. "Can't find him anywhere," she said as she looked right, then left. She was a little out of breath. "Where did he disappear to?"

Mitchie laughed.

"What's so funny?" Jenelle asked.

"He's right behind you," Mitchie told her. "Hey, Anderson!"

We all turned just in time to see Anderson standing with Kiwi. They both looked up, surprised — almost as if they'd been caught doing something.

Jenelle hesitated, but Mitchie waved. "Over here, you guys!"

Kiwi and Anderson looked at each other, then walked over slowly. "Hi," Anderson said. "What's up?"

"Jenelle was looking for you," Mitchie announced.

"Yeah." Jenelle twisted a lock of her blond hair

around her finger. "I just wanted, to, uh — I wanted to let you know that I won't be able to come over later. I know we had plans, but my mom needs my help at the store —"

"Oh, no problem!" Anderson said brightly. Then he looked at Kiwi and smiled. Kiwi smiled back, then looked away.

Jenelle looked from Kiwi to Anderson, then back again. As I looked at her face, I felt a knot tightening in my stomach. I wanted to say something, but I didn't know what. Anything. Anything to break the tension.

Why don't I know any jokes? I wondered desperately.

"Oh, great — you're all here." Preston elbowed his way through the crowd, which spat him out right in front of us. "Just the people I need to see. Okay, official prank meeting in the library after school. You all have to be there." He pounded his fist into his palm. "If the seventh grade doesn't pull something better than this stupid fire alarm prank, I swear that I will *die* of shame."

Jenelle winced. "I can't today."

Anderson shook his head. "Sorry, man."

"Yeah, me neither," Kiwi agreed.

More awkward silence.

"I'll be there," I heard myself say.

"You *will*?" Preston looked like a kid on Christmas morning. "Amy Flowers, I knew you'd come through!"

What did I just do? I thought. I didn't want to help with the prank. But at that point, I would have said just about anything to end the awkwardness between Anderson, Jenelle, and Kiwi.

"I'll be there, too," Mitchie offered. She looked at me and nodded.

Did she just say that to end the awkwardness between us? I wondered. I wasn't sure if I cared, though. I didn't want to be the only one working on the prank with Preston, that was for sure.

"This is awesome! Our prank is going to rock!" Preston did a funny little jig in a circle that made him look borderline insane but made everyone laugh.

Which made me want to hug him.

Preston grinned at me, and I felt my face get warm.

"Whoa — you've got the serious Bozo the Clown cheeks," Preston teased. "Where's your big red nose?"

And, just like that, my urge to hug him was over, and I wanted to strangle him instead. Typical Preston.

*   *   *

I peered through the crowd milling around the auditorium. It was two hours later, and the Senior Serenade was about to begin. The seniors were onstage, seated on risers. They seemed cocky and confident, elbowing one another and grinning. After a year of looking stressed out and exhausted, they could finally relax. Most of them had been admitted to the colleges of their choice — Yale, Vassar, Duke, Vanderbilt, Stanford, Rice — and all of them were finished with finals and only had to pick up their diplomas at the end of the week. I envied them. I was finished with finals, too . . . but I still had to deal with the stress of Preston and the prank.

"Looking for something?" Fiona asked as she and Lucia traipsed up the wide aisle to the center section, where the seventh and eight grades were supposed to sit. A couple of girls I knew slightly — Ivy and Pear — were following in the League's wake, like eddies in a stream. "Did you lose your friends?" Fiona gave me a smug smile. "I guess that's what happens to losers."

"Yeah, like, losers lose things?" Lucia echoed. "And they, like, get lost?"

Ivy and Pear snickered, then Pear leaned over to whisper something in Fiona's ear.

I ignored them, even though I *was* looking for my friends. I'd stopped at the girls' room on the way to the Serenade. Now I didn't see Kiwi, Mitchie, or Jenelle anywhere.

But my silence didn't have any effect on Fiona. "Speaking of losers — way to ruin the seventh grade's shot at winning the Serenade, Amy," she said. Her gold bangles jingled as she raked her elegant fingers through her long, glossy hair. "Thanks to your one vote, we're stuck with *Preston's* song." She made a little noise in her throat as if she had a hairball caught in there.

Something about that irked me. I mean, it's not like I was the *only* one who voted. "Whatever, Fiona. I think we've got a funny song."

Then something really weird happened. Lucia harrumphed and tossed her long, bouncy brown hair over her shoulder. She pursed her lips and said, "Yeah, and I think the stomping and clapping is, like, fun?"

For a moment, Fiona's face was perfectly still. With her pale skin and fine features, she looked like a marble statue. Then clouds gathered in her blue eyes, and her dark brows lowered. "What?"

Lucia shrugged. "I voted for Preston's song, too," she said — without a question mark.

Pear whispered something to Ivy. Her pale blond hair covered her lips as she was speaking, but I could hear what she said. "Me too."

Fiona's blue eyes flicked toward Pear, then back to Lucia. "I can't believe you voted against me." Her voice was low, like the rumbling of the earth before an avalanche.

Lucia took a deep breath and folded her arms across her chest. "Like, not everything is about you, Fiona?"

Have you ever seen a lit fuse — you know, in a movie or something? It smokes and hisses as it sparks its way toward dynamite. Well, Fiona looked like that.

"Wow, I just remembered that I have to be — somewhere else," I said quickly. I turned and ran directly into Preston.

"Just the girl I wanted to see!" he said with a grin. Tugging my hand, he pulled me down into the seat beside his.

"They're going to start any minute," I told him, craning my neck to see if I could spot Mitchie or my other friends.

"Eh, these things never start on time," Preston replied. "Do you like roller coasters?"

I cocked my head. I wasn't sure I'd heard him right. "What?"

"Roller coasters." He waved his hands in dramatic loops, as if to illustrate what he meant. "You seem like the kind of person who likes zooming around. All of my other friends hate them. The last time we went on the Sky Claw, Anderson nearly screamed my ear off."

"Yeah, I like them," I said. This is something of an understatement. Actually, I *love* roller coasters. All kinds — from the baby ones to the loop-de-loops. "Why are you asking? Are you conducting some kind of poll or something?"

Preston laughed. "No! I just have a couple of season passes to Five Mountains. I thought maybe we could go this summer. If you're going to be around."

Five Mountains is a theme park located at the center of Houston. I'd been there exactly once — with Fiona and Lucia, of all people. I'd been dying to go again, but I wasn't sure I'd be able to afford it. But here was Preston, offering me a ticket.

He grinned so widely that I noticed two of his bottom teeth were growing in at an angle — practically overlapping. Like they were fighting for space in his mouth. Maybe all of the words that were constantly pouring out made it crowded in there. It was surprisingly cute.

I was so busy thinking about Preston's teeth that I guess I didn't respond right away, because Preston's smile kind of faltered. "I mean, if you don't want to go, it's okay. It's just that a lot of my friends are going to be out of town, and I'm stuck here —"

"No," I said. Preston looked kind of crushed, so I added, "I mean, yes. I'd love to go. That sounds like fun."

Preston grinned. "Yeah, doesn't it?"

I nodded. It really did. Preston was kind of crazy, but I had to admit that we usually had a lot of fun together. We were actually becoming . . . friends. I laughed a little, and Preston laughed, too. He was about to say something when someone called my name.

"Amy!" Scott shouted as he made his way down the aisle. "There you are! Oh, excuse me," he said as he squeezed past a group of girls seated at the end of the row. "I've been looking all over for you. Oh, hey, Preston. Mind if I sit here?"

Scott didn't wait for an answer — he just plopped into the empty seat beside me. I was in the middle of a Scott-Preston sandwich. "So!" Scott said brightly.

We all smiled at one another, but nobody said

anything. For some reason, I felt like a complete idiot.

"Ready for the Serenade?" Scott asked after a moment. "The eighth grade has a killer song."

"Ours is really good, too," I said quickly. "Preston came up with it."

"Yeah?" Scott smiled politely. He didn't really seem that interested.

Preston squirmed uncomfortably. "It's okay. It should be funny."

"Hey, speaking of funny — how did you guys like that alarm earlier?" Scott's brown eyes gleamed. "Pretty good prank, right? My buddies pulled that." He pursed his lips and nodded at me as if he expected us to be impressed.

Preston didn't say anything. Which I thought was pretty kind of him, given that he'd gone off on how lame the prank was.

"It was really nice to be out in the sunshine," I volunteered.

"Yeah." Scott stretched the word out into kind of a sigh and reached his arms over his head. He leaned back in his chair and laid his arm across the back of my chair. A small smile danced at the edge of his lips.

It was weird. Scott was my crush, but having his arm lying on the seat back behind me made me feel kind of like an insect pinned to something. I felt trapped. And embarrassed. *Why is that?*

Preston was eyeing Scott's arm as if it was a snake. Like he wasn't sure what his next move should be.

"Do you think they're ever going to get started?" Scott leaned forward in his chair to look over at Preston.

When he leaned forward, his arm fell partly onto my shoulder. That seemed to make up Preston's mind. "Yeah — I think they are. Actually, I should go find my friends." He stood up awkwardly and gave me a smile. "See you later, okay?"

I wanted to ask him to stay, but I didn't dare. *He probably feels like a third wheel,* I figured, and I didn't blame him for ducking away. That was one of the worst feelings in the world. "See you," I said as Preston hurried off.

"What's later?" Scott asked.

"Oh, we're going to plan our class prank," I explained.

"*You* are?" Scott's eyebrows shot up.

Irritation burned through me. "Why are you so surprised?"

He shrugged. "You just don't seem the type."

"What type am I?" I heard the annoyance in my own voice, and I was surprised. I mean, I actually even *agreed* with Scott. *Preston* was the only person on earth who thought I'd be a good prank-planner. *Why am I attacking Scott?*

"I don't know," he said. "The not-planning-a-prank type." He laughed.

Just then, the lights started to dim and Headmistress Cardinal walked onstage. The audience erupted into cheers as she stepped up to the microphone.

"Here we go!" Scott said brightly. "Get ready to sing!"

"Finally," I muttered.

He smiled at me, and I felt a wave of guilt. The fact was, I couldn't wait for the Serenade to get started because I didn't really feel like talking to Scott anymore.

I didn't like to admit it, but sometimes Scott just wasn't that much . . . fun.

CHAPTER SIX

Amy's Prank-Planning Rule #1: If it seems impossible, it probably is.

I could hear the chatter from the library's Austin Room by the time I was halfway up the stairs. The Allington Library is an enormous space with a huge three-story wall of windows at the front. There is a bunch of smaller rooms up the back stairs on the second floor where clubs and book groups can hold meetings. Each of the rooms is named after one of Texas's great heroes, like Sam Houston, James Bowie, and Stephen F. Austin. Preston had told me to meet him in the Austin Room. It was one of the smallest but also one of the nicest, with a view of the main school building and black-and-white prints on the walls.

70

When I walked inside, I saw that all of the chairs around the dark wood oval table were filled — clearly, Preston had been on the warpath recruiting people for the prank. He was talking to Don when I walked in.

"But where would we even get one?" Preston was asking. He looked kind of annoyed.

"Dude — my uncle's farm!" Don replied. "I'm telling you, it'd be hilarious!"

I tapped Preston on the shoulder and he turned around. "Oh, hey," he said. "You came." He sounded a little distracted and a little cool — almost as if he didn't really care whether or not I came. "You can just find a seat anywhere. We're going to get started in a minute." Then he turned back to Don. "I just don't think it's really practical. . . ."

Disappointment flickered in my chest. *Well, what did I expect — that Preston would faint with joy the minute he saw me or something?* I thought. *Actually — come to think of it — he usually does kind of go bananas whenever he sees me.* He'd usually shout out "Amy Flowers!" or find some special way to bother me. I guess I was starting to get used to it.

Mitchie waved at me and pulled her turquoise hoodie off the chair beside hers.

"Thanks for saving me a seat," I said as I slid into the chair. "It's more crowded than I expected." Naturally, Emmett had tagged along with Don. Fiona was chatting with Lucia and tapping her fingernails against the sleek wood of the table. A few other kids were seated directly across the table from me, including Brooke Rosen. She gave me a wave, and I smiled back. She was class president and a really cool person.

"Preston's got a lot of friends," Mitchie replied.

I nodded, even though I was a little surprised. I mean, Preston can really drive me crazy sometimes. But looking around the room, I realized that maybe I was the only one who felt that way.

Preston clapped his hands. "Okay, let's get started," he announced, and the room quieted down. He stood at the head of the table, a thick black marker in his hand. "I thought we'd take the first few minutes and just toss around some ideas. I'll write them all down on this whiteboard." He gestured behind him. "Then we'll see if anything jumps out at us as the best."

Don's hand punched the air. "I've got an idea!"

Preston sighed. "Okay, Don — tell everyone." He waved the marker at his friend.

"Okay!" Don grinned and looked around the table. "Get this — we put a *cow* on the roof!"

"Dude, that's awesome!" Emmett gave him a high five.

The rest of the table was quiet.

"Um — how would we get a cow onto the roof?" Brooke asked finally.

Mitchie wasn't as polite. "Are you nuts?" she snapped. "Even if we *could* get a cow onto the roof, the poor thing would be terrified. And what if it fell off?"

Emmett looked horrified.

"Great point, Mitchie," Preston said quickly, sounding relieved. "Okay, any other ideas?"

"Dude — you're not even going to write 'roof cow' up on the whiteboard?" Don demanded.

Preston gave him a look that nearly cracked me up. I had to pretend to cough into my hand to cover my laughter.

"Next?" Preston asked.

"Maybe we could set off some fireworks in the hallways?" Emmett suggested.

"Um, I think that's illegal," I told him.

"And a fire hazard," Preston added. "Next?"

"Maybe we could have pizzas delivered to a few classrooms," Brooke suggested.

"Good one!" Preston turned to write it up on the whiteboard. "If we pay in advance, they'll have to accept them." Soon, the ideas were starting to flow — a guy named James suggested that we could get the entire seventh grade to start coughing and sneezing at the same time. Preston said we could change the time on the clocks in all of the classrooms. Someone suggested that we could steal Mr. Pearl's coffee cup.

"I think that might be more dangerous than setting off fireworks," Preston said, and everyone laughed.

I smiled. I was actually surprised at how well Preston was handling the meeting. I'd assumed that he'd have a bunch of really elaborate prank ideas, but so far he just seemed interested in hearing what everyone had to say.

"Maybe we could send around a memo telling the teachers that there's a special meeting for them during fourth period," Emmett piped up.

Preston nodded. "We could make it look pretty official," he said as he added it to the list.

Fiona let out a loud, elaborate yawn.

Preston lifted his eyebrows at her. "Yes, Fiona?"

"Oh, nothing," she singsonged as she pulled her glossy black hair over one shoulder. "It's just that these pranks are incredibly boring. And didn't the ninth grade do the clocks thing last year? I was hoping that the seventh grade would come up with something a little more original, that's all."

"Cow on the roof!" Don shouted.

"Did you have something in mind?" I asked her. *Or do you just want to put down everyone else?* I added mentally.

"As a matter of fact, I do," Fiona purred. She toyed with the gold bangles stacked on her wrist. "I think we should plant bluebonnets on the golf course." A smirk crawled up the side of her face. "They could spell out 'Seventh Grade Rules!'"

"Sounds like a lot of work," Preston said, but he wrote it up on the whiteboard.

"No, wait," I called.

Preston turned to look at me, the marker hovering over the board.

"It's just — it's illegal to dig up bluebonnets," I pointed out. They're the official state flower of Texas, and there are laws protecting them. "The school would have to leave them there forever."

Fiona rolled her eyes. "That's the *point*, Amy."

"Yeah, like, the point is that they'll still be there when we graduate?" Lucia chimed in.

"Awesome!" Don cried. "Only — instead of flowers — we should use cement!"

"Gerardo would freak," Mitchie murmured. She looked concerned, and I didn't blame her. The groundskeeper is a really sweet man, and it seemed unfair to make him the prank's main victim.

"I thought we wanted to do something funny," I said. "Not destructive."

Fiona snorted. "Can you stop being a goody-goody for five minutes?" she demanded.

"Yeah, you just keep sitting there, shooting down other people's ideas," Emmett snapped. "You're a pain."

"I'm not trying to be," I told him. "I like the idea of doing something that says 'Seventh Grade Rules.'"

"That's a good point," Preston agreed. "There are so many pranks on Friday, sometimes it's hard to know who's pulling them. We don't want the eight grade stealing credit for our brilliance!"

"Oh, I know!" Fiona sat up straight and batted her eyes sarcastically. "We could send flowers to all of the teachers along with a note that says 'With love from the seventh grade!'"

"Yeah, and maybe we could give them, like, gift certificates?" Lucia added.

I gritted my teeth. "I'm not *that* much of a kiss-up."

Fiona made a wet smooching sound. I didn't strangle her, even though I wanted to.

"Look, maybe we could do something else that screams 'seventh grade,'" Mitchie suggested.

"Like what?" Fiona demanded.

"Like . . . maybe we could print up a bunch of bookmarks," I said. "We could leave them in the library books."

Fiona waggled her finger in the air limply. "Whoop-de-do. Bookmarks."

"No, I mean, like, *hundreds* of bookmarks," I said. "All over the library — people will be finding them for years."

An excited murmur ran around the table. Fiona looked around in surprise as Preston wrote it up on the board.

"I really like that!" Preston said. "They could say 'You've been buzzed by the seventh grade!'"

"I could get them printed?" Lucia suggested.

Fiona glared at her.

"Like the invitations you did for Beach Day?" Brooke asked. "Those were so cool!"

"Oh, yeah, those were great!" The room exploded with compliments. Lucia beamed, while Fiona looked like she wanted to rip something to shreds.

"Okay, it looks like we're into this idea," Preston said as he punched a hand into his pocket.

"The only problem with it is that it's a little quiet. People may not even notice that we've done it until next year, when they start checking out books again. I'd like to also do something that catches people's attention on Friday."

"What if we hid alarm clocks all over the school?" Mitchie suggested. "We could set them to go off every thirty seconds."

"Yeah — we could create half an hour of complete chaos!" Emmett crowed.

"I love it!" Don chimed in.

"All those in favor?" Preston asked.

The room chorused with yesses . . . except for Fiona. She sat, tight-lipped, in her chair, her arms folded across her chest. Mitchie grinned, and I gave her a high five.

"Okay, we'll need some folks to show up early on Friday to pull the prank," Preston said.

"What time?" Brooke asked.

"Five thirty?" Preston said, and the room let out a collective groan. "Hey, I'll be here," he protested. "You can't all wimp out on me!"

"I'm in," Mitchie said.

"We'll be here," Emmett said as Don grunted in agreement.

Preston looked at me. "Sure," I said slowly. "I think I can make it." I knew I'd have to ask my parents, of course, and I wasn't sure what they'd say. . . . Still, now that I'd been in on the planning, I didn't want to miss out on making the prank happen.

"Anyone else?" Preston asked.

Fiona huffed. "Fine."

"Okay. Then I think we're all set." Preston erased the whiteboard and joined us as everyone started gathering their things. "I knew you two evil geniuses would come up with something great," he said. He was looking at me when he said it.

"We weren't evil enough for Fiona," I pointed out.

Preston shrugged. "Not much point in trying to keep her happy."

"Tell me about it," Mitchie agreed. "Her idea of a great prank is one where someone ends up expelled or crying."

I laughed. My heart was thudding as Preston's clear eyes sparkled in delight. For some reason, this prank meeting had left me feeling giddy and light-headed.

I never realized that I liked pranks so much. I guess Preston was right all along.

"Hey!" Jenelle beamed at me from my kitchen table. She was sitting there, slicing lemons in a very crowded kitchen. My parents were there and so were hers.

"Amy's home!" Uncle Steve wrapped me in a hug so big that it actually lifted my feet off the ground.

"I'd forgotten you guys were coming over for dinner," I said as Steve placed me gently back on my feet.

"You're a little late, aren't you, Amy?" Mom looked at me over the top of her glasses. She's a major worrier.

"Sorry," I said, swiping a carrot slice from the salad Linda had just arranged. "The prank committee meeting lasted a little longer than I thought it would."

"The what committee?" my mom asked just as Uncle Steve crowed, "You're planning pranks without *us*?" Their faces were like a page from a child's book on opposites. Uncle Steve looked delighted. And Mom looked . . . well, the opposite of that.

My dad poked his head up from the herbs he was chopping. "What's the prank?" he asked, grinning hugely. Mom flashed him a frown. He cleared his throat and dropped his smile, although I could still see it hiding in his eyes. He and Uncle Steve exchanged a look. "Ahem."

"Honestly, Ernest," Mom snapped. "Amy, you know that if you get another detention, it could mean a real problem for you."

"It's okay, Mrs. Flowers," Jenelle piped up. "The pranks are school-sanctioned activities."

"Really?" Linda lifted an eyebrow at her daughter.

"Well, mostly." Jenelle bit her lip. "Kind of," she corrected.

Mom looked doubtful. "By 'kind of,' do you mean 'not really'?"

"Nobody has ever gotten into trouble for pulling a prank during Crazy Week," I said. Preston had told me that. "Unless it's dangerous. And we're not planning anything bad."

"Not going to drive the dean's car out onto the old football field, eh?" Uncle Steve asked, and he and my father hooted with laughter.

Jenelle and I looked at each other. She gave me an I-have-no-idea shrug.

"Guess you won't be holding a water pistol fight in the cafeteria!" My dad held up his palm, and Uncle Steve high-fived it.

"Um . . ." I glanced at Linda, whose eyebrows were wrinkled in confusion. Clearly, she had no idea what those guys were talking about, either. "I think I speak for everyone when I say — huh?"

"What's this?" Uncle Steve gaped at Dad, wide-eyed. "You've never passed on the stories of your legendary pranks to your daughter?"

"What?" I giggled at the thought of my father — the Man in the Sweater Vest — pulling pranks. He gave me a smile that was half sheepish, half proud. "Mom? Is this true?"

My mother rolled her eyes and went back to chopping her carrot. "Your father used to be a major practical joker," she said.

"And Uncle Steve was my accomplice!" Dad announced.

"Except for the time you locked me in my room." Uncle Steve laughed heartily. "I had to tie my bedsheets together to climb out the window!"

Dad waved his hand. "You lived on the first floor."

Uncle Steve winked at me. "It still seemed like a long way down."

"Oh, my." Linda shook her head. "I'm glad I didn't know you two in college."

"You don't know the half of it," Mom agreed.

"Amy, your father and I are ready to help you in any way we can." Uncle Steve gave me a low bow. "When it comes to pranks, we're at your service!"

"Absolutely!" my father agreed.

Mom sighed loudly. "Really, Ernest, I don't think we should be encouraging —"

"I'm sure Amy isn't doing anything destructive," Dad said quickly. "Are you, Amy?"

"Of course not." I was glad that the committee had managed to stop Fiona before she dug up the golf course. I decided it was time to change the subject. "So! What time is dinner?"

"Are you finished with those lemons, Jenelle?" Dad asked. She nodded. "Good. The fish needs to bake for about an hour."

"You girls can go upstairs for a while, if you want," Mom said.

Jenelle washed the lemon juice off her hands and we headed up to my room. Jenelle picked up a photo that was sitting on my desk. It was of all of us — me, Mitchie, Jenelle, Kiwi, and Anderson. Preston had taken it at this food festival we'd all gone to. Then he'd printed it out and given it to me. Which was a pretty nice thing for him to do, come to think of it.

For some reason, the thought of Preston sent a shiver through me. I didn't feel like talking about him, so I latched on to the first alternate subject that popped into my mind. "Can you believe your stepdad and my dad were such lunatics?" I asked.

"Hmm?" Jenelle looked up from the photo. "What?"

"Steve and my dad," I said. "Who knew they were pranksters?"

"Oh, yeah." Jenelle placed the picture back on my desk — facedown, I noticed.

"Are you okay?" I asked. "You look a little green."

Jenelle trudged over to my bed and flopped onto the edge. She looked up at the ceiling. "Amy, have you noticed that Anderson is acting a little . . . weird lately?"

"Definitely not," I said — way too fast.

Jenelle looked at me sharply, and I felt my face heat up. Then she sighed. "I think he's about to break up with me."

"No . . ." I sat beside her and took her hand. "No — he wouldn't. He's crazy about you." I really meant it. Even though I had to admit that he *had* been acting weird. He actually even seemed *happy* when Jenelle canceled their plans earlier. Bi-zarre.

Jenelle looked me full in the face. "Then why is he spending so much time with Kiwi lately?" Her hazel eyes were large and soft, like she really hoped I had an answer to that question. Which I didn't.

84

Just then, my door slammed open and Kirk burst in. I'd never been so happy to see my brother in my life, even though he was scowling and pointing a finger in my face. "Hi, Kirk," I said.

"Hi, Kirk!" he mimicked in a high-pitched voice. "Hi, Kirk! I'm so happy to see you, Kirk! I'm going to hand out lousy advice and ruin your life, Kirk!"

I gaped as he sashayed around my room in what I guess was an insane imitation of me. "Is everyone in this house drinking crazy juice?" I asked him.

"I just got off IM with Alizae!" Kirk snarled. "I asked her to go to the end-of-year dance next week, and do you know what she said? Do you? Do you? Do you have any idea?"

"No," I said.

"That's right!"

"What's right?" I asked. I'd meant, "No, I have no idea," but Kirk had taken it the wrong way.

"She said no!" Kirk yelled. "She said that she liked being 'just friends.' Just friends! After we went to the movies together!" He stomped around, looking like he wanted to throw something. Finally, he settled for an old magazine. "Aargh!" Kirk tossed it into the air. It fluttered to the floor, and he kicked it.

"Why are you punishing that magazine?" Jenelle asked.

The question actually seemed to calm him down a little. "We went to the movies together, Jenelle," he said as if that explained everything. "I mean, wouldn't you call that a date?"

"I guess," Jenelle admitted.

Kirk turned on me. "Thanks a lot, Amy," he said sarcastically. "It's your fault that I asked her out in the first place. That's the last time I'll take advice from you!" And he stormed out.

Jenelle stared at the closed door for a moment. "Wow," she said.

"I know — welcome to my crazy family," I told her.

"No, I mean —" Jenelle shook her head. "Does Mitchie know that Kirk asked out Alizae?"

I studied her face. Jenelle looked concerned. "She knows," I admitted.

Jenelle bit her lip. "I just hope she's not too crushed out."

"Mitchie told me that she *didn't* have a crush on Kirk," I said slowly.

Jenelle's eyebrows lifted in a flicker of surprise. She recovered, but a pink blush was crawling up her neck. "Oh," she said quickly. "Um, hey —" Jenelle looked around the room, and her eye fell on my floor. She bent over to grab the magazine as if it was a life preserver. "What do you think of this weird argyle craze? Isn't it just completely ugly? Mom thought we should get some for the store, but I said that I thought it would be over in about five minutes, right?"

I looked down at the magazine. My legs felt slightly wobbly, as if I'd just stepped aboard a boat floating in rough seas. My head was swimming with thoughts. *Why did Mitchie tell Jenelle about her crush and not me? Not only that — she actually lied about it when I asked her.*

Sure, maybe she was embarrassed, but didn't she trust me? Weren't we friends?

But I didn't say any of that. "I've never been crazy about argyle," I told her.

CHAPTER SEVEN

Amy's Love Feast Rule: Save room. You'll need it.

Where are my friends? I wondered as I poked my head into the Fern Room. The Allington cafeteria isn't just one large warehouse-style space, the way it was at my old school. Instead, it's made up of several different, smaller rooms, and Mitchie, Kiwi, Jenelle, and I usually met up for lunch in the Sunflower Room. But when I went to our table, I saw that it was empty. They weren't in the Freesia Room, either, and I knew Mitchie would never eat in the Rose Room — she said the shade of pink on the chair cushions made her want to lose her lunch. I glanced around the Fern Room. Scott was there with his friends, but he had his back turned toward me. I was actually kind of glad. We were supposed to be going to a movie later that night, and for some reason I felt a little embarrassed. I didn't really want to go over and talk to him in front of his friends. I don't know — I just felt like there might be a lot of *grinning*. And nudging one another. And I just didn't want them to think of me as "that girl Scott is going out with." Not yet, anyway.

My friends weren't there, either, so I ducked out and headed down the hall. There was only one place left to investigate — the Dahlia Room. It was a beautiful room, painted a dark shade of maroon and trimmed in black. A large crystal chandelier hung from the center of the ceiling, casting soft light on the plush velvet chairs. The large windows overlooked the smooth green Allington golf course. It was probably the loveliest room in the entire school, but I always found it a little unwelcoming. Maybe because the League always ate there.

"...and Order by Numbers will be playing?" Lucia was saying as I poked my head through the doorway. The League's table was unusually crowded. I knew that Fiona only liked to eat with her close friends, but today a group of stylish seventh grade girls had clustered around Lucia.

They were pointed toward Lucia like compass needles, eager to catch her every word. "My uncle is, like, their lawyer? So they're going to play a set?"

"Awesome!" Pear Waters didn't usually smile much, but right now her face looked like a beam of sunshine. "I *love* that band."

"They're really amazing," one of the other girls agreed, and soon everyone had chimed in.

Fiona stabbed at the salad on her plate. "Whatever — their lead singer always sounds like he has a cat stuck in his throat," she said.

But I'm not sure Lucia even heard that comment, because she was already waving at me. "Amy?" she called. "Hey, Amy — come on over? I've been, like, looking for you?"

I wondered briefly how she could have been looking for me while she was sitting in her usual chair, but I decided against mentioning it. I walked over and plunked my tray at the end of the table as Lucia dug around in her oversized suede hobo bag. Fiona didn't look up from her plate. She just chewed the bite she'd taken. Chewed and chewed, grinding the particles into nothing, I suppose.

Finally, Lucia pulled out a small cardboard box. She crooked a finger at me, telling me to come closer. I stepped up behind her and she pulled out a bookmark. "I had these printed up?" she said, pulling one out of the box. It was printed on lavender paper with raised blue glittery letters. It looked really cool.

"I love it," I said, reaching for the strip of paper.

Fiona plucked it from my fingers. "Lavender?" She sneered, flipping it over. "And this side is completely blank. Don't you think it's a little girly? And — *blah*?" She smirked and tossed the bookmark back into the box.

I expected Lucia to get mad or cry or something, but instead she just said, "Yeah, I know what you mean? When I saw them, I was like, bo-ring?"

Fiona smiled triumphantly.

"So I also made these?" Lucia went on, and she pulled out another box. Inside were yellow bookmarks printed with black glittery letters. "I thought it worked better with the 'you've been buzzed' idea?" Lucia flipped over the bookmark. A small black-and-yellow glittery bee sparkled on the back.

"Gorgeous!" I said as I held it up. "I'll bet people will go around *trying* to find these!"

Fiona just grunted. She looked like she was

about to make a snide remark, but Pear said, "Pass them over," and soon the box had traveled around the table. "What are they for?"

"Can I keep one?" one of the girls asked.

"We, like, need them for the prank?" Lucia said.

With a disappointed groan, the girls passed the bookmarks back. Lucia was smiling proudly as she handed them over. "Do you want to show them to Preston?" she asked me.

"Sure," I told her. I tucked the box into my bag. "I'm positive he'll love them."

Fiona poked her fork into a cherry tomato, and it squirted all over the front of her dress. "Oh, great," she snapped. *"Perfect."* She tossed her silverware onto the plate with a clatter. She dipped her napkin into her water glass and dabbed daintily at the green raw silk. "This is probably ruined."

Lucia lifted her eyebrows at me and I gave her a little wave as I walked out of the room. I actually felt a little sorry for Fiona. She was having a rough day. Well, a rough day *for her*. For me, spilling something on my dress and having my good friend talk about the cool party she was planning didn't really sound like a life-ruiner.

I headed back through the main food area. Still no sign of Mitchie, Kiwi, or Jenelle. *Where have they disappeared to?* I wondered. *You'd think that one of them would be there! Maybe they're looking for me, too. . . .* I pictured myself and my three best friends wandering through the maze of Allington's cafeteria rooms, all looking for one another, for the rest of the lunch hour. I'd just decided to head back to the Sunflower Room and wait for them to show up when I turned a corner and spotted Kiwi at the end of the hall. She was with Anderson. I couldn't hear what they were saying, but Kiwi's face was lit up like the night sky on the Fourth of July. She wrapped Anderson in a huge hug.

I wanted to look away, but I couldn't. I felt queasy as I stood there, watching them. *Jenelle was right*, my mind whispered.

It was almost as if Anderson heard me, because just then, he looked over. "Amy," he said as he blushed and jumped away from Kiwi. "Hey, I'll — I'll see you later, okay?" Running a hand through his blond hair, he turned and walked away. He was moving so quickly that he whacked into the door frame with his shoulder, but he didn't stop. He just kept moving.

"Hey, Amy," Kiwi said. I tried to read her face. *Does she look guilty? Nervous? Embarrassed?* I couldn't tell. Mostly, she just looked happy. "Sorry

I'm late for lunch. I just had to talk to Anderson about something."

"Kiwi — what's going on?"

She pressed her lips together. "What do you mean?" she asked carefully. Her eyes held mine for a moment, then flicked away.

An image of Jenelle's face flickered through my mind. She'd looked so sad last night. I really needed to know if her worries were silly — or not. "I mean with Anderson," I explained. "What's with all of the whispered conversations and getting together?"

Kiwi fidgeted, raking her fingers through the tips of her waist-length hair. "We're friends."

"You're not acting friendly," I pointed out. "You're acting like someone who's keeping a secret."

Kiwi looked at me in surprise. She hesitated a moment, as if she wasn't sure how to respond. "I just —" She paused. "I ran into Anderson at the mall last week. He told me that he had this . . . problem. I'm just helping him figure it out."

I didn't want to press . . . but I felt like I needed to know. "What kind of problem?"

Kiwi bit her lip. "It — it's about a girl —"

My stomach sank. That wasn't really the

94

answer I'd been hoping for. I was about to press Kiwi for details when a voice cut me off.

"Hey, there you two are," Jenelle said as she walked up to us. "Our table is empty!"

Kiwi's lips clamped together. She flashed me a don't-say-a-word glance, and I felt queasier than ever.

Jenelle poked my arm. "Come on! I'm starving," she said.

I looked down at my food. It was pasta primavera — one of my favorites. Salad. And one of the famous Allington macadamia white chocolate chip cookies. But I could hardly face sitting down at a table with Jenelle and Kiwi when I knew they were keeping secrets. "You know, I really don't feel hungry," I said.

"Saving room for the Love Feast later?" Jenelle teased. "I hope you brought the popcorn balls."

"Of course," I told her, faking a smile. "Actually, I've got something I need to show Preston. So maybe I'll catch up with you later?"

"Sure," Jenelle said, and Kiwi nodded.

"Hey, can I have your lunch?" Kiwi added. "I'm starving."

I handed her my tray, and she and Jenelle walked toward the Sunflower Room. *Maybe they'll work everything out while I'm gone*, I thought as I headed for the exit.

I wasn't really too hopeful, though.

I was on my way to the library when I saw them. Preston was standing with Mitchie at the end of the hall. They were both laughing.

"You're brilliant!" Mitchie said.

"It was your idea," Preston told her, and then he put his hand on her shoulder.

It's hard to explain how I felt at that moment. Once, when I was visiting my cousins in Connecticut during December break, Kirk sneaked up behind me and nailed me in the back of the head with a snowball. Cold, powdery snow exploded down the back of my neck like a pouf of talcum powder. Then it melted, slithering down my spine and sending a damp shiver all over my body. As I looked at Preston's hand on Mitchie's shoulder, I felt like I was reliving that snowball. I felt that same wet shiver.

Just turn around, I told myself.

But my feet were like stones. They were heavy — I couldn't even drag them in the opposite direction.

And then it was too late. Mitchie saw me and nearly jumped a mile in the air. She hurried to step in front of something, and Preston's hand dropped off of her shoulder.

He turned to face me, eyes wide. "Oh!" he said, the fear on his face melting away. "It's just Amy."

I wasn't sure how to take that ("*just* Amy"), but Mitchie was already walking toward me with a warm smile. "You've got to see what we've got." She grabbed my hand and dragged me toward Preston.

"Check it out," Preston said as he picked something up off the floor. It was about the size and shape of a cat, only it was made of silver metal and had a very short tail. Preston pressed a button and placed it back on the floor. After a moment, the thing let out a high-pitched beeping noise and galloped down the hallway.

Mitchie laughed. "Isn't that awesome?"

"What is it?" I asked as the thing crashed into a set of lockers and turned to gallop in a different direction.

"It's a Clockbot," Preston explained. "You have to catch it before you can turn it off."

"This is going to cause absolute craziness," Mitchie said. "Preston's got forty of them."

"Forty?" I turned to Preston. "What did you do, spend your life savings on Clockbots?"

He laughed. "I told Anderson about the prank

we're planning, and he got them for us. His dad invests in the company." He laughed as the Clockbot careened into a wall. It actually turned a flip and raced back toward us. I had to jump out of the way to keep from getting stepped on.

"Oh, hey, speaking of pranks . . ." I pulled the box of bookmarks out of my bag. "Lucia had these printed up."

"Cool!" Mitchie said when I gave her one. "These look really great. Love the bee."

I turned to Preston, who was still watching the Clockbot's antics. "What do you think?" I asked. I held up a bookmark.

"Hm? What? Oh, nice." His head pivoted as the Clockbot galloped by. "Gotcha!" He grabbed it and pressed a button. He chuckled. "Aren't these amazing? I'm cracking up imagining them all going off every thirty seconds! The teachers will go nuts."

Click, click, click, click, click. The kitten heels on Fiona's alligator shoes clacked against the marble floor as she strode up to us. "Preston, there you are," she said. "Look, I wanted to talk to you about the bookmarks —"

"Yeah, Amy showed me." Preston dropped the Clockbot back into its box. "They look fine."

Fiona rolled her eyes. "They look *dumb*," she announced. "That whole prank is dumb. I think we should go with the bluebonnets."

"Forget it, Fiona," Mitchie snapped. "Face it — your prank lost, okay?"

Preston straightened up and looked her in the eye. "Mitchie's right," he said. "We all agreed on the other pranks. It wouldn't be right to just over-rule what we all voted on. Besides, there's no time. We're pulling the prank tomorrow. Which reminds me . . ." He turned to me. "Amy, did you ask your parents if you can definitely get here early? I was thinking you'd be the perfect person to put on bookmark duty."

"No problem," I said, thinking about my dad. I'd asked for his help after dinner the night before — when Mom wasn't around. Naturally, he'd agreed right away.

Fiona planted a hand on her hip. "Well, *I'm* not helping," she announced. "Not if we're doing this lame prank."

"So what else is new?" Mitchie grumbled.

"Fiona, believe it or not, we don't really need your help," Preston told her. "We've got a bunch of people to help hide the clocks. I'll just ask Lucia if she can help Amy take care of the bookmarks."

"Lucia?" Fiona's voice was shrill. "That girl will get caught in thirty seconds. You should have seen the way she was waving around the bookmarks just now! 'Hey world,'" she mocked, twirling her long hair Lucia-style. "'I'm, like, pulling a prank?'"

I shook my head. Lucia was Fiona's best friend. I couldn't believe she would just make fun of her that way.

But Preston didn't bat an eye. "I'm not worried," he said.

"Fine — I'll help," Fiona said. Then she turned and stalked away.

"Man, she is so annoying sometimes," Mitchie said.

"Eh." Preston looked at the ceiling.

"How can you put up with her?" Mitchie asked.

"I don't know," he admitted. "I just always feel like Fiona *could* be really cool . . . if she could get over herself. Anyway, she'll help out. That's the thing about her — if she says she'll do something, she does. But — we do have one problem. . . ."

"What is it?" I asked. It actually seemed like Preston had things pretty well organized.

He jammed a fist into his pocket. "I don't actually know how we're going to get into the school before it opens," he admitted.

Mitchie let out a little laugh. "No problem," she said.

"Really?" I asked. The mischievous twinkle in her eye was actually making me smile. It was infectious.

She nodded. "Just leave that part to me."

CHAPTER EIGHT

Amy's Date Rule #2:
It's always best to avoid strangling the person you're on the date with. No matter how crazy he makes you.

"Look out!" someone cried as a leather ball winged toward my head. I ducked, and a handsome dark-haired guy chased after the ball. His red-and-blue-striped rugby shirt stood out boldly against the vibrant green grass. I'd stepped into the middle of the park's green field without thinking, and somehow I'd wandered smack into the middle of a rugby game.

"Good reflexes!" Scott trotted up to me, wearing a wide grin. His shirt was yellow and navy, and his sandy-blond hair was damp with sweat. "Maybe we should get you to join the team."

"If the game is about ducking away from the ball, then I'm sure I'd be great at it," I joked.

Scott laughed. "Thanks for meeting me here. Just give me a second." He turned and trotted onto the field. "Hey, guys, I've got to head out!" he called.

The rest of the boys turned to look, and I realized with a sudden chill that the guy holding the ball was Preston. He gave me a little wave.

I waved back, feeling suddenly shy as Preston jogged over. "Hey, Soda Pop," he said.

I shook my head. "What?"

He nodded at my outfit. I was wearing a flowy white cotton sundress. "You look like a soda commercial," Preston explained. "You know — fresh and clean in that white dress, standing on the green grass under the blue sky."

I knew I was blushing all over. I actually felt the tips of my hair turn warm as he reached out and tugged one of my curls.

"Doink!" Preston grinned as it sprang back into place.

I giggled, then grimaced at how screechy and nervous I sounded. *What is wrong with you?* my brain yelled. *It's just Preston — get a grip.* I thought about slapping myself across the face but decided it would just make things worse.

I noticed that Preston was the only guy who wasn't wearing a rugby shirt. Instead, he had on a ratty old pale-blue T-shirt that read, "Elvis's Automat" in bold black letters across the front. "What's that?" I asked him.

Preston looked down at his shirt. "Oh, my older sister's in this rock band. The name is goofy, I know — but they're really good."

I laughed a little. It was sort of cute to think about Preston supporting his sister's band. *He really can be sweet sometimes*, I thought, and then felt myself blushing again. *Stop blushing!* I commanded myself, which — of course — only made things worse.

"Hey, thanks for waiting," Scott said as he hustled over. He'd pulled a pair of jeans on over his shorts, and had exchanged his cleats for Vans. A messenger bag was slung across his chest. "Sorry I'm still wearing this shirt. I guess it's your turn to hang out in public with someone who's all sweaty and gross!" He laughed a little, but I winced. Scott had a slight smudge of dirt on his sleeve and his cheeks were pink from exercise. Basically, he looked like a preppy catalog's idea of Athletic Guy. On the other hand, after Field Day, I'd looked like something that had escaped from the town dump. *Thanks for reminding me,* I thought.

I half expected Preston to make some kind of sarcastic comment, like, "Yeah, Amy's used to looking gross," but instead he just asked, "Where are you guys off to?" He tossed the rugby ball into the air casually.

"We're going to see *Football Rock Star*," Scott said.

"Cool!" Preston said. "I've been dying to see that! Mind if I come with?"

"Sorry, man," Scott said. "I bought the tix online. It's probably sold out now."

Preston looked at me. "Oh," he said.

I gave him a little smile. My body was swimming with a crazy stir-fry of feelings. I felt embarrassed to be on something that looked like a date with Scott. And I was a little mad at Preston for asking if he could come along. And I was a little disappointed that he wasn't going to come along. And I felt like an idiot for wearing a dress. And I wanted to smack Scott for saying "tix" instead of "tickets," like a normal person.

What is wrong with me? I wondered. Preston was looking at me, and I felt like I was melting. Like I was on the verge of disappearing into the grass in a small, smooth puddle, like the Wicked Witch of the West after Dorothy nailed her with a bucket of water.

"Hey, Preston!" a tall guy with red hair called. "You in?"

"Yeah. Yeah, sure." Preston turned back to us. "Well, have fun," he said. He gave Scott a gentle punch in the arm, then jogged back onto the field.

"He's a cool guy," Scott said as we started toward the edge of the park.

I forced myself not to look back at Preston. "Yeah," I agreed. "He is."

"Whoa," Scott said as we joined the massive herd of people trooping into the movie theater. "I knew it would be crowded, but this is crazy! It's a good thing I bought the tix ahead of time."

What do you want, a medal? I thought, then immediately felt bad. *Why am I feeling so grumpy?*

We found good seats, and Scott settled back into his, slinging his arm casually across the back of my seat, like he had just before the Senior Serenade. It made me squirm.

"I think I'll run to the ladies' room before the movie starts," I said, slipping out of my chair.

"I'll save your seat," Scott promised.

I squeezed past a group of teenage boys and made my way up the aisle. When I pushed open the heavy ladies' room door, I was greeted by a wall of backs. A group of girls was clustered at the makeup mirror, brushing their hair and applying their lip gloss. It struck me as a little funny, since they were clearly about to go sit in darkness for about two hours. I almost laughed, but then I heard a familiar voice say, "It's going to be way better than last year's?" It was Lucia. She was standing at the center of the group — Ivy and Pear were on either side of her. "And the swag bags are going to be so much cooler than Fiona's?"

"You mean it'll be better than a chocolate bar in the shape of Fiona's head?" one of the girls asked, and everyone laughed.

"That was the dumbest party gift ever?" Ivy agreed. "Although it was kind of fun to bite into Fiona's head." Everyone snickered.

"It'll be, like, way better?" Lucia fluffed her bouncy waves. "Here's a little hint — hope you need a new phone!"

The girls squealed.

"It's going to be, like, amazing?" Ivy chirped.

Pear rubbed her lips together and checked her teeth. "I can't wait to hear the band?"

Whoa — now everyone's, like, talking like Lucia? I thought. Then I caught myself. *Wait — did that thought just sound like Lucia, too?*

"Oh, Amy!" Lucia smiled as she turned around to face me. "Are you, like, ready for our big prank tomorrow? It's going to be amazing?"

The other girls murmured in agreement.

"Yeah," I said. "I think everything's all set." I looked around.

"Great? I'll, like, see you later?" Lucia laughed. "We've got to get back to our seats before someone wrestles them away from Imani?"

Imani? I thought. *Who's that?* I realized it must be someone from the sixth grade. It looked like Lucia was making some new friends. "Where's Fiona?" I blurted.

Lucia's back went rigid. She pursed her lips. "At home, I guess?" she said. "I have, like, no idea?" She frowned a little testily. "It's not like we do everything together?"

It's not? I thought.

"Yeah, like, Lucia's not in charge of Fiona's whereabouts?" Pear chimed in.

"Oh. Right." I was fighting a serious feeling of déjà vu. It was like now Lucia had her own Lucia — someone to agree with whatever she said in question format. *Weird.*

"See you later?" Lucia said, and she flounced through the door. The rest of her little flock swirled behind her.

I turned to the mirror, as if I expected to see traces of Lucia there. Instead, I just saw my own face — confusion stamped across my features. And something else.

I'd been wondering why I'd been feeling so bad for Fiona. Why — when she was such a lousy friend to me? But now I knew the answer. It was because I knew that Fiona trusted Lucia. She thought she was her friend.

But neither of those girls knew how to be a friend. They wouldn't know a real friend if she came right up to them and gave them a hug.

And that was just plain sad.

"I'm starved," I said, flipping through the over-sized laminated menu. It was the kind that had photos of the food along with tempting descriptions that ended in exclamation points, like, "Sizzling with chipotle sauce, this burger will tantalize your taste buds!" I flipped to the back page. "Everything looks good."

"Especially the desserts," Scott said, picking up the special menu that the waitress had left by the ketchup. "Wait — I shouldn't even look at that yet." He set it back in its place.

Something about the prim way he put the dessert menu back on the table annoyed me. "Why not?" I asked, picking it up and paging through the fudgy, the fruity, and the creamy. My stomach let out a low rumble. The movie had been a lot longer than I'd expected, and by the time we left, Scott and I were both hungry for dinner. Luckily, the next day wasn't a "real" school day — just pranks and class parties — so Mom had said that I could stay at the mall until eight thirty. "Maybe I'll order dessert first," I said playfully.

Scott laughed, but he didn't look up from his menu. "Right," he said.

Irk! That *irked* me. An image of Preston eating a banana split popped into my mind. Once, we'd gone out for lunch together, and he'd gotten dessert first. At the time, I'd thought he was crazy. I'd even given him a mini health lecture about it. But I'd hung out with Preston enough since then to know that he actually ate pretty healthy most of the time. My lecture must have seemed pretty annoying. *I hope he didn't find me as irky as I find Scott right now*, I thought suddenly.

Just then, the waitress walked up to our table. "Hi, I'm Caitlyn and I'll be taking care of you tonight," she said. Her voice was kind of a monotone, as if she'd said that five thousand times already that evening.

"Hi, Caitlyn," I said. "I'm Amy, and this is Scott."

Caitlyn blinked at me, as if she hadn't expected me to jump in with my own name. "Oh — hi." She shook her head a little and smiled. "Um — do you want to hear our specials?"

"I think I know what I want," Scott said, folding his menu. "I'll have the Big Tex burger without the jalapeños. That comes with a salad, right? I'll have ranch dressing."

Caitlyn wrote that down. "And what would you like, *Amy*?" She put a little extra emphasis on my name, as if it amused her to use it.

"Well, Caitlyn, I think I'd like the Fudgeosaurus," I told her. "And I guess I'll have a taco salad, too. But I'll have the vinaigrette dressing."

"A health nut, I see." Caitlyn gave me a wink. "Coming right up."

"You're getting a chocolate brownie sundae for dinner?" Scott asked once Caitlyn had disappeared.

"Well, I guess I'm having the salad for dinner," I told him. "It's just that I'm going to eat dessert first." I grinned at him, waiting for a laugh, or at least a smile or something.

Scott frowned. "That's not good for your teeth."

I sighed, deciding to change the subject. "What did you think of the movie?"

"Pretty good," Scott said.

I waited for a second to see if he would say something else, but he didn't. "I really liked the songs," I volunteered.

He toyed with the paper coaster sitting beneath his water glass. "Some of them were kind of dorky," he said.

"Like which ones?"

"That one where all of the football players sing during practice." He leaned back against the padded booth and scoffed. "Like that would ever happen."

"I liked that song," I said.

"I'm just saying that football players wouldn't dance all over the field like that," Scott insisted.

"Well, I guess that's kind of the point," I said. "It was a musical. It's not supposed to be realistic." Scott didn't reply and then Caitlyn brought out our food, thank goodness.

"Bon appétit!" she said brightly. "Amy and Scott."

"I've never had anyone introduce me to a waitress before," Scott said as he squirted ketchup onto his burger. "It's a little weird for her to know my name."

"We know *her* name," I pointed out.

"Yeah. But isn't that just so that we can call her over if we need her?" Scott put the top of the bun back onto his burger and cut it in two neat halves.

"I don't know," I replied. *I just thought it was because she was a person*, I thought — although I didn't say that.

I dug a spoon through the mountain of whipped cream sitting on top of my sundae. "Mmm," I said as chocolate melted over my tongue. The ice cream was putting me in a better mood already.

Scott chewed for a moment. "I wonder what your friend thought of it."

"Hm? What?" *What friend?* I wondered. *What are we talking about?*

"Your friend — the one sitting in the back row of the movie. I wonder what she thought of the song."

"You mean Lucia?" I asked.

Scott nodded. "Yeah, I think that's her name. The one surrounded by look-alikes."

I laughed a little. "That's her. I have no idea what she thought of it." I pushed away my sundae and took a bite of my salad. The fresh, bright taste of warm grilled chicken and greens bit through the sugar coating on my tongue. "She's not really my friend," I added after a moment.

"I thought I'd seen you guys together," Scott said. "At school sometimes."

"I don't know — she can be kind of ..." I searched for the right word. "Well, backstabby, I guess." I told him about our conversation in the restroom, and about Fiona.

"They sound like jerks," Scott said.

"They are, sometimes," I admitted.

"So why do you care about them?" Scott asked.

"I don't," I said.

Scott cocked his head. "Then why are we talking about them right now?"

I fought the urge to point out that *he* had brought them up. The fact was, he had a point. I *did* care. *Why?* "Well ... I guess I see them at school all the time...." This was true. We were like planets that kept coming into one another's orbits. But I knew that wasn't the whole story. My mind flashed back to something Preston had said once. "Fiona could be really cool ... if she could get over herself," I said slowly. It was kind of true. And it made her hard to give up on.

Scott finished his burger and brushed off his hands over his plate. "Maybe," he said. "But she's never *going* to get over herself. So forget it."

I swirled my long-handled spoon through the hot fudge in my half-eaten sundae. I didn't really want the rest of it. And the salad was better for me, anyway. So why did I want to have just one more bite? It's like Fiona, I realized. Sweet sometimes, but nothing you could live on.

Still — it's hard to get rid of. Hard to stop picking at.

I was about to say these things to Scott, but I could see from the expression on his face that his mind had already moved on to something else. Oh, well. I mean, this is a guy who never would have ordered the sundae in the first place, right? He just didn't get it.

In some ways, he just didn't get *me*.

Scott tipped his head to look into my face. His eyes were as deep and chocolatey as the hot fudge sauce in the bowl before me. "Hey," he said softly as he lifted his right hand toward me. He stroked my chin with his thumb, and I felt as if I'd been dipped in warm fudge myself.

Scott pulled back his hand. "Chocolate sauce," he explained, holding up his thumb. "You had a little dribble."

"Oh, thanks." I quickly wiped my face with my napkin.

"I was tempted to leave it there," Scott admitted. "It was cute."

I wondered how he could say something like that without blushing when I felt like my face was something I could use to warm my hands on. He smiled, flashing those perfect teeth, and my heart thudded and skipped.

He doesn't get me, I thought, but it didn't stop my heart from racing.

It didn't make sense — how could I have a crush on a guy who just didn't understand where I was coming from?

I guess sometimes I don't get me, either.

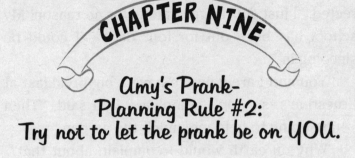

CHAPTER NINE

Amy's Prank-Planning Rule #2: Try not to let the prank be on YOU.

"Stop whistling," Kirk demanded as our father guided the minivan through the dark Houston streets. "You can't whistle along to a Coldplay song — it's ridiculous."

"But it's so catchy!" Dad insisted.

Kirk groaned. "It's five o'clock in the morning! How can you be so cheerful?"

"Because we're going to have some fun!" Dad glanced at me in the rearview mirror. "Right, Amy?"

"Um, technically you're just dropping me off at school," I pointed out. "But, you know, if you think that's fun . . ."

"Of course it's fun," Dad replied. "We're playing a small yet vital role in the big prank!"

"I'm not playing a role in the prank," Kirk corrected. "I just got dragged along for no reason. My school has been out for four days — I could be sleeping in."

"You and I are going to have a big breakfast at Ernestine's, so don't complain," Dad said. "Then you're going to help me mulch the garden."

"Why on earth would I complain about that?" Kirk asked sarcastically. He shot me a dirty look.

I couldn't really blame him. Our dad loves getting up early and doing chores, and he thinks that "rousting Kirk out of bed at a decent hour" is "character-building." Luckily, Dad usually only goes chore-bonkers about once a month. Dad also pays Kirk for the work that he does, so it's not like he's suffering. But that never stops him from complaining.

By the time we reached school, the sky had brightened from black to purple-gray, and the sun was starting to light clouds with pinkish-gold at the edge of the horizon. The entrance to Allington was well lit, so we could see that a couple of people were standing at the gates. Preston was there. So was Fiona. Mitchie was talking to Gerardo through the gate. A moment later, it swung open.

Kirk sat up a little. "Mitchie's in on the prank?" he said. "Man, Amy. I can't believe your cool friend is doing something this early in the morning — which is so very *uncool*."

"Do you need any help?" Dad asked as I popped open the side door. "Is there anything else we can do?"

I smiled at him. He looked so eager to be in on the prank that I actually wished there *was* something for him to do. "I think we'll take it from here," I said. I patted him on the shoulder. "Thanks, Dad."

"Good luck," he said.

"Perfect timing," Preston said as I climbed out of the minivan.

Mitchie held up a set of keys. "Gerardo says this big one will get us into the library. The rest are for classrooms."

"Okay, let's hide most of the Clockbots in rooms on the seventh grade hall," Preston suggested. "Mitchie, you and I can take care of that, along with whoever else shows up. Amy — you and Fiona can handle the bookmarks. You brought them, right?"

"Sure," I said, just as Fiona said, "Excuse me, why do you need a bunch of people for the Clockbots and only two for the bookmarks?"

"Because we have to program the alarms and hide the clocks," Preston explained. "It's more complicated."

Fiona sighed, as if having to hide the bookmarks was the worst torture ever. Still, I had to give her credit. It was five twenty A.M., and she was here. And her hair and makeup were perfect. She must have gotten up at four to make sure she was keeping it glam.

We hurried over to the library, and Mitchie unlocked the door for us. Inside, the space seemed even more enormous than usual. Light was beginning to glow through the three-story windows, but darkness gloomed down the rows and rows of library books. I reached for a switch on the wall.

"Don't," Fiona snapped. "We'll get caught."

I nodded. Of course. If we flipped on the lights, any teacher who came in early would see that something was up. We would just have to deal with the semidarkness. I shuddered a little at the thought.

"You guys all set?" Mitchie asked. "I'll be back to help as soon as we're done with the bots."

"We're good," I told her. Mitchie gave me a playful punch on the arm. The double door made a heavy *ker-chunk* as it closed behind her.

I pulled out the box of bookmarks and handed half over to Fiona. "I'll handle fiction," she said, pointing to the section near the circulation desk. "You can get non."

I glanced over toward the far wall, where the nonfiction and reference books were located. It was the darkest part of the library. A shiver skittered up the back of my neck. *There's nothing there but books,* I told myself, but still — that darkness gave me the creeps. "Why don't we both do fiction?" I suggested. "I think it makes more sense to have a bunch of bookmarks in a popular section than just a few in books that nobody will check out."

Fiona looked at me carefully. "Okay," she said at last. "Fine. I'll take A through J."

I took a deep breath, surprised at how relieved I felt. "Sounds great," I told her. I decided to start at the end of the alphabet. "I'm going to stick a bunch in the Harry Potter books," I said.

"Great idea." Fiona's voice floated toward me. She was only a few rows away, but I still wished she was closer. It wasn't completely dark in this section of the library — but it wasn't that light, either. I had trouble reading the titles on the spines and had to lean close to see what I was doing.

"We should really concentrate on the most popular books," I said, pulling down a title I'd read last year. I knew it was on the sixth grade reading list, so I dropped a bookmark in the center, then slid the book back into place. "The stuff that'll get checked out first, you know?"

"Mmm."

"I mean, what's the point in putting bookmarks in some of these books that nobody's going to read, right?" I knew that I was babbling, but I couldn't seem to stop. Hearing my own voice was comforting in the dim light. "I mean, you can kind of tell which titles are the most popular, just because they're the ones that are the most beat-up. I'm just going to skip anything that looks too perfect, you know? Fiona?"

I stood still. The library was silent.

"Fiona?" I called.

Nothing.

Click.

What was that?

My breath caught in my throat — my tongue felt like it was made of cotton. I felt my lips form the word "Fiona," but it came out as a whisper. *Don't think about vampires*, I commanded myself, and immediately my mind was crowded with monsters from the movie Kirk had been watching two nights ago. *Vampires don't exist*, I told myself.

That's what people in horror movies always say before they get eaten, said another part of my brain.

I hate my brain sometimes.

"Fiona?" I called again.

I heard a low scraping noise — the *exact* kind of noise a zombie would make. It sounded like it was coming from the far wall, near nonfiction. I froze.

"Fiona!" I shouted. If I hadn't been so afraid, I might have been struck by how happy I would have been to see Fiona at that moment — given that I'm usually so unhappy to see her in normal life.

The silence dragged on, and then — *clang!* "Ow!"

Ow? Okay, one thing I know about vampires — they never say "ow." There was another clang followed by a thunk, and I followed the noise to a doorway that I hadn't noticed before. I knocked. "Fiona?"

"Amy!" she cried. Her voice was muffled through the door. "Let me out of here!"

"What is this?" I asked, trying the doorknob.

"It's a broom closet," she said.

"It's locked," I told her.

The door rattled as if she was trying the knob from the other side. "What?" she shrieked. "Get me out of here!"

"Why are you in a broom closet?" I asked.

"Who cares?" Fiona screeched. "Let me out!"

"I'm trying," I told her. "But I'm telling you — it's locked."

"It must've locked behind me," Fiona said with a groan. "Amy — you have to get me out of here!" *Thud! Thud!* She was pounding the door with her fist.

"Why did you go in there in the first place?" I asked, shaking my head. It didn't make sense. *Was she looking for the restroom or something?*

Fiona growled. "I was going to play a trick on you, okay?"

"A trick?" I repeated.

"I was going to jump out and scare you." Fiona's voice was a little strangled. "But now *I'm* scared — it's dark in here!"

I folded my arms across my chest. "Well, that's what you get for —"

"Spare me the lecture," Fiona snapped.

My mouth clamped shut. "Okay," I said after a moment. She was being punished enough, after all. "Okay, I'll go get Mitchie."

"No," Fiona said. "Don't leave me."

"But how am I supposed —"

"Don't leave me alone here in the dark," Fiona begged.

I fought the annoyance rising in my throat. *This is just my luck — to get stuck with Fiona.* Mitchie is off with Preston. They're probably having a great time, laughing their heads off about the Clockbots. *And here I am, Fiona's babysitter.* Still, I couldn't just abandon her. I knew I'd be totally freaked out if I was locked in a dark closet.

"All right." I sat down with my back against the door. "So . . ." I said after a moment. "What are you doing this summer?"

"Who cares?"

"You want to just sit here in silence in the dark?" I demanded. "Fine by me."

It was quiet for a moment, then Fiona said, "I'm going to visit my aunt's family. They have a house on this Greek island. It's right on the beach."

I thought about my summer plans, which were basically to hang out and do a lot of babysitting for our across-the-street neighbors. Somehow, Greece seemed more glamorous. Just a teensy bit. "Wow, that sounds amazing."

Fiona snorted. "I guess. My parents send me there every year. But the house is over three hundred years old and the rooms are really small and sometimes there isn't enough hot water to have a long shower."

"It still sounds amazing," I told her. Actually, that description had made it sound even *more* amazing.

"I guess it is really pretty," Fiona admitted. "Have you ever been to Greece?"

"I've never been anywhere outside of the United States," I told her.

"Really? Not even to Paris?" she asked. As if Paris was, like, the mall and everyone dropped by at least once a week.

I laughed. "Not even there."

"Oh, you have to go," Fiona gushed. "It's such a beautiful city! And the fashions are amazing. Everything is gorgeous there — it would blow your mind."

"One day," I said.

"Yes," she said.

We were silent for a moment. Maybe it was because the sun had risen even more, but the library didn't look as gloomy as it had earlier. "How are you doing in there?"

"I'm okay," Fiona said. Then, more quietly, "Thanks for staying."

Thanks? I thought. *Fiona said thanks?* I didn't even know how to reply.

Just then, the double doors burst open. "How's it going in here?" Mitchie's voice echoed through the library. "Where are you guys?"

"Over here!" I called.

Mitchie saw me and hustled over. "Hey, we have to get going. The teachers are already swarming the halls. Where's Fiona?"

I gestured with my thumb over my shoulder. "Locked in."

"Locked in?" Mitchie repeated. "What is that — a broom closet?"

"She was going to jump out at me," I explained. "And she got locked in."

"Mitchie! Let me out of here!" Fiona cried.

Mitchie's eyes narrowed. "She was going to scare you? That's nice." She held out a hand and pulled me to my feet. "Let's go," she said.

"Wait — we have to let Fiona out," I told her.

"We have to?" Mitchie asked. "Really?"

"Mitchie!" Fiona screeched. "Don't you dare leave me here! You will be so sorry! I'll make you miser —"

"Oh, spare me, Fiona," Mitchie shot back. She pointed at the door, as if she was having an argument with the wall. "You've already made me miserable. You cut off my hair. You've humiliated me over and over again. Give me one good reason that I shouldn't leave you in there."

"You wouldn't," Fiona said.

"I'm not as nice as Amy," Mitchie pointed out.

"You have to let me out of here!" Fiona cried, pounding on the door. "You *have* to!"

"Mitchie, we can't just leave her in there," I said in a low voice as Fiona raged on.

"I know," Mitchie said, pulling the key out of her pocket. "But Fiona's the one who loves to pull tricks, right? I'm sure she won't mind a taste of her own medicine." She waited an extra moment before she put the key in the lock and yanked the door open.

Fiona stumbled out, mid-pound. She looked up at Mitchie, her face stamped with surprise.

"You're right, Fiona, I wouldn't just leave you in there," Mitchie said. "I may not be as nice as Amy, but I'm not like you, either." She cocked her head at me. "Come on, I have to get the keys back to Gerardo."

She started toward the door.

"Mitchie," Fiona called.

Mitchie stopped, but she didn't turn back. "What?"

"I'm sorry," Fiona said.

Mitchie's back was as still as stone. "What for?"

"We were good friends," Fiona said slowly. "Weren't we?"

"Yeah." Mitchie's voice was heavy, like a tree falling. "We were." Then she walked through the doors.

Fiona looked up at me, but I didn't know what to say. I felt sorry for her then — really sorry. The expression on her face told as much as the books that lined the shelves nearby. For the first time, Fiona realized what she had lost when she threw away her friendship with Mitchie. And I think she regretted it.

Maybe she regretted what happened with me, too.

Gong.

The golden tone of Allington's class bell rang through the crowded hallways. Students were milling around, chatting and gathering their notebooks for the last day of classes.

"Here we go," Mitchie said, flashing me a mischievous smile.

A loud beeping blasted from the nearby English classroom, and a moment later, a Clockbot scampered out. Laughter exploded and a small circle opened up around the Clockbot as it dashed into the crowded hallway. One girl screeched and jumped out of the way.

"What is it?" someone shouted.

"Get it!" cried another.

At that moment, another series of beeps tore through the hall as a purple Clockbot raced out of the math classroom. Everyone shrieked and laughed as they scrambled to get out of the way, raced after the Clockbots, or simply tried to get to class.

"Preston Harringford is a demented genius," Mitchie said as another Clockbot escaped.

I smiled, wondering where Preston had disappeared to. I knew he had to be watching the fun from somewhere.

"Out of the way! Out of the way! Out of the way!" Mr. Pearl shouted as he raced after an escaping Clockbot. He reached toward the beeping alarm with one hand and kept the other tightly wrapped around his commuter mug. "Someone get that thing!"

Mitchie giggled, and he pulled up short in front of her. His huge eyes bulged out of his head in an expression that looked like a fine blend of annoyance and amusement. "Michiko Ohara, you wouldn't have anything to do with these rampaging robots, now, would you, hmm?"

Mitchie blinked innocently. "Define 'anything.'"

"There it goes!" An eighth grade boy raced past, closing in on a Clockbot just as two more dashed around the corner. "Stop them!"

I couldn't help it — I laughed. Mr. Pearl chuckled a little, too. "We'll discuss this later," he said as he hurried down the hall to capture a Clockbot.

"Got one!" A tall, gangly guy with a shock of blond hair held up one of the robots and shut off the beeping noise.

"It's going into the science lab!" A girl pointed as another bot dashed toward Mr. Pearl's room.

"Why didn't I shut the door?" Mr. Pearl wailed from the other end of the hall.

I turned to take a step toward the classroom, but someone chasing a Clockbot ran right into me — headfirst.

"Oof!" I fell on my butt — hard.

The Clockbot-chaser did, too. He looked up at me in surprise as the robot smashed into the wall, then darted away in the opposite direction. "I didn't see you."

It took me a moment to realize that the person sitting in front of me in the middle of the hallway was Scott. He gave me a smile as I rubbed the spot on my side where he'd accidentally head-butted me. "Are you okay?" he asked. "Sorry — I wasn't looking."

"No permanent damage," I said, forcing a smile at him.

"Enough lounging on the marble floors," Mitchie said as she held out a hand. "You don't want to get trampled by a crazy alarm clock," she said as she hauled me to my feet.

Scott stood up and brushed himself off. His head swiveled as a Clockbot dashed past. "Listen — I've got to catch one of those guys. I made a bet with one of my friends. But I'm glad I ran into you." He laughed at his own joke. "And — hey — I had a great time last night."

"Oh, me too," I said. *That doesn't really count as a lie*, I told myself. *Okay, so it wasn't technically a "great" time. What does "great" even really mean?*

A Clockbot beeped by.

"See you later!" Scott darted off.

"Ooooooh . . ." Mitchie punched me in the arm. "He had a *great* time last night!" She winked one eye, then the other.

"Yeah." I clutched my notebook to my chest uncomfortably. I really didn't want to talk about it.

"I can't believe it took this long for you to mention it!" Mitchie cried. She poked me in the arm. "You've been holding back!" She poked me again.

"Like you should talk," I shot back.

Mitchie's face froze and I covered my mouth with my hand. We stood there like two trees rooted to the floor as chaos swirled around us. Mitchie's eyes searched mine, and I could tell that she knew that I knew about Kirk.

"Did Jenelle tell you?" Mitchie asked after a moment.

I winced. I didn't want to cause a problem between my friends. "She thought I knew."

Mitchie sighed. "I knew that would happen," she said.

"Why *didn't* I know?" I asked.

Mitchie looked away. "I don't know. . . . I guess I was just . . ." She shook her head. ". . . embarrassed."

"Hey." I touched her shoulder. "We're friends."

She nodded. "Yeah. But Kirk is your *brother*. That would have been weird."

"Well . . . a little," I admitted.

"You think he's gross," Mitchie went on.

"I don't think he's *gross*," I said.

Mitchie gave me a look.

"Okay, sometimes he's gross," I admitted. "But he can also be nice. And the point is — we're friends. We don't keep secrets."

"I guess I thought it didn't matter." Mitchie tucked her short, glossy bobbed hair behind her ear. "I mean, he's in high school. It wasn't going to happen."

"True," I said. Around us, things were starting to quiet down. The eighth grade boys had made a game out of catching the Clockbots, and they'd gotten most of them. "Then again, we'll be in high school in two years."

Mitchie shuddered. "Don't talk about it," she said. "First we get to enjoy being eighth graders. We're going to rule the school." She held up her hand for a high five, and I slapped it, laughing.

"Girls?" A dark-haired teacher motioned to us. "Let's get along to class."

Mitchie and I fell into step, side by side. The hallways were starting to empty out.

"You know, Kirk actually referred to you as 'my cool friend,' this morning," I remembered suddenly.

Mitchie's eyebrows flew up. "Really?"

I nodded. "Really."

She smiled. "Cool."

"And things didn't work out with Alizae," I went on. "Which is kind of sad —"

"— but not really," Mitchie finished, and we both laughed.

Mitchie slung her arm around me. "I'm glad you found out," she said.

"Me too," I told her. I put my arm around her shoulders.

And we walked down the hallway just like that.

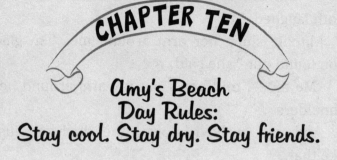

CHAPTER TEN

Amy's Beach Day Rules: Stay cool. Stay dry. Stay friends.

"What do you think they're talking about?" Jenelle whispered as she cast a suspicious glance toward Kiwi, who was standing beside the drinks table with Anderson. "He's leaning toward her — no, wait — he's just getting a glass of orange soda. What's she laughing at? Oh, she spilled cranberry juice on herself." Jenelle nipped at her cuticle, twisting her finger nervously.

"Jenelle." I put a gentle hand on her shoulder. "You. Must. Chill."

"Oh, I'm chill. I'm very chill. I'm so chill I'm *cold*," Jenelle insisted. "I'm subarctic. I'm hanging out with penguins. I'm —"

"Okay, maybe you need to thaw," I told her. "Look, it's a beautiful day. We're hanging out by the beach. Take a look around you." I gestured to the wide green lawn bordered by rows of palm trees. Close by was the large Spanish-style stucco mansion that was Lucia's family's beachfront getaway. She had set up a stage near the wide steps that led to the rear entrance to the house. Tables of drinks and snacks were arranged under a shady trellis. It looked like the entire seventh and eighth grades had turned out for the unofficial ending of the Allington school year. "Why don't you try to have a good time?"

Jenelle looked dubious.

"What is this, National Misery Day?" Mitchie asked as she joined us. She was holding a plate of fresh vegetables and hummus dip.

"Okay, I'm not *that* miserable," Jenelle insisted.

Mitchie looked surprised. "I wasn't talking about you." She nodded over to a palm tree that was set a little apart from the others. Fiona was seated beneath it, sipping a glass of sparkling water. She looked elegant there in her long blue sundress. But she couldn't hide the fact that she was alone.

"Should we go join her?" I asked after a moment.

Nobody said anything.

Fiona must have felt our eyes on her, because she looked up. She flashed me a dirty look, then turned her face away.

Mitchie sighed. "I'll bet she's having a rough day. This used to be her show."

A peal of laughter cut across the lawn. Lucia was seated at the top of the steps to her house, surrounded by adoring groupies.

"Queen for a day," Jenelle mused.

Mitchie nibbled a carrot. Then she cleared her throat. Without a word, she started walking toward Fiona.

I don't really know why, but Jenelle and I followed.

A frown flashed across Fiona's face as we approached. She placed her glass on the ground and stood up to face Mitchie. "Are you lost or something?" She looked at Jenelle, tossing her hair and sticking out her chin. I'd never seen Fiona look so defensive.

Mitchie just looked at her. "You tell me," she said.

Fiona was silent for a moment, as if weighing her options. Finally, the hardness in her face melted slightly. She gestured toward the ground beneath the palm tree. "Want to sit down?" she asked.

138

Mitchie smiled and plopped on the soft grass.

Jenelle gathered the hem of her peach sundress and tucked her legs beneath her as I settled down beside her.

"Dip?" Mitchie asked, holding out a baby carrot with a bit of hummus on the tip.

Fiona looked surprised, but she accepted the carrot. She took a dainty bite. "It's good," she said.

"Lucia's family knows food," I pointed out.

Fiona winced a little. "Yeah."

I noticed that Jenelle's head was twisted toward the drink table. "Where did they go?" she asked, half to herself.

"Who?" Fiona asked.

Jenelle looked pained.

"Anderson and Kiwi," I explained.

"I'm sure they'll find us," Fiona said. "It's not *that* big a party."

Jenelle shook her head. "I can't stand this," she announced. "I've got to break up with him."

"What are you talking about?" Fiona demanded. "Break up with who? Anderson?" She looked from my face to Mitchie's as if she expected to see an explanation written there. "Why?"

"Because I think he's about to break up with me," Jenelle admitted.

"That's stupid — why would he do that?" Fiona took another carrot from Mitchie's plate and dipped it in her hummus before taking a bite. Mitchie flashed her an amused look but didn't say anything. I guess she'd finally gotten used to people stealing her food. "Anderson worships the ground you walk on, Jenelle. Breaking up with you wouldn't even cross his mind." She munched the carrot decisively.

"You think so?" Jenelle asked, and I smiled. I was actually pretty surprised that Fiona would defend Anderson. After all, she had tried to break up Jenelle and Anderson a couple of times.

"Definitely. He's a sweetheart," Fiona said. "He'd never do anything sketchy behind your back."

"Listen to Fiona." Mitchie leaned back on her elbows. "She's right."

Whoa — Fiona admitted she was wrong about Anderson, and Mitchie is taking her side. I checked the sky, just to see if there were any flying pigs. A couple of puffy white clouds floated across the crystal blue, but that was it.

"Jenelle?" A hesitant voice asked. It was Anderson. Kiwi was right behind him. They had padded up behind us so softly that we hadn't even heard them coming. Anderson looked at the ground shyly, his arms behind his back. "Can I talk to you?"

I saw Jenelle's chest rise and fall in a deep breath. The smile that lit up her face a moment ago had winked out. "Sure," she said . . . but she didn't sound sure.

Anderson glanced at us, then corrected himself. "Privately?"

Jenelle went white, and her hand reached for mine. "Anything you have to tell me, you can say in front of my friends." On the word "friends," she shot a dagger glance at Kiwi. But Kiwi didn't notice. She was looking at Anderson, who had turned to her with his eyebrows raised. Kiwi nodded encouragingly.

My body was cold. I felt like the ice sculpture sitting at the center of Lucia's drinks table. I couldn't breathe. I couldn't move — I was too terrified of what was about to happen. Jenelle's fingers felt as cold as mine.

Anderson glanced at me and blushed a little, then he seemed to make a decision. He pulled something out from behind his back. It was a box. It was painted deep midnight blue and had small silver stars pasted all over it. "This is for you," he said.

Jenelle released my hand and slowly reached

for the box. She stared at it as if she couldn't make sense of what was happening. I really couldn't, either. It was the strangest way of breaking up with anyone I'd ever heard of.

Jenelle flipped open the lid. Inside, her own face smiled up at her from a photo taken in the fall. She was standing with Anderson, and they had their arms wrapped around each other. Jenelle picked up the photo. There was another one underneath. This one was of all of us — me, Jenelle, Anderson, Preston, Mitchie, and Kiwi. The box was full of pictures. Photo after photo of Jenelle, Anderson, and all of our friends. When she took out the stack of pictures, I saw that "Remember" was painted at the bottom of the box in gold letters.

Jenelle stood up to look Anderson in the eye. "What is this?" she asked.

"It's a memory box," Anderson explained. "I . . ." He hesitated, then looked over at Kiwi, who smiled. "Jenelle, I don't know how to tell you this, but . . . my family is going to spend the whole summer in Alaska."

"Alaska?" Jenelle whispered.

Anderson's eyes were bright. "I just wanted to make you something so that — so that you wouldn't forget about me."

"You're going to Alaska?" Jenelle repeated.

"We're leaving in two weeks. And I'll be back the second of August." He held out his hands. "I know it's a long time. . . ."

Jenelle looked down at the box. "And you *made* this?"

"Kiwi helped," Anderson said quickly. "She helped a *lot*. I know it's not perfect — there's a spot in the corner where I smudged it —"

But Jenelle cut him off with a huge hug. "It's wonderful," she whispered. "It's *perfect*."

Anderson gave Kiwi a thumbs-up over Jenelle's shoulder, and she beamed. I felt a wave of heat wash over me — I couldn't believe I'd ever thought the worst about Kiwi and Anderson. They were the sweetest people I'd ever met. How could I have ever thought otherwise?

I have the best friends in the world.

"Well, that solves that," Fiona said, munching another one of Mitchie's carrots. "But what's the big deal, Anderson? You're only going to be gone for eight weeks."

Anderson cocked his head at Fiona. Then he turned to Jenelle. "Do you want to take a walk or something?" he asked.

"Sure," she said warmly. She cast a grateful look at Kiwi, then looked down at her box. Jenelle and Anderson strolled off together, flipping through photos and chatting.

"It's so great to make someone happy!" Kiwi said as she plopped onto the grass beside me.

Mitchie and I exchanged a glance. I could tell from the expression on her face that she was thinking the same thing I was — that we should just skip telling Kiwi how miserable she'd made Jenelle for the past week.

"Omigosh, Fiona, like, I've been looking all over for you?" Lucia darted up to us, panting. The confident smile she'd been wearing moments before had disappeared. "I, like, need your help? I'm having an emergency?"

"Oh, really?" Fiona didn't sound too interested.

"Order by Numbers is here?" Lucia said.

"Oh, I love that band!" Kiwi said happily.

Lucia glared at her, then turned back to Fiona. "And, like, they were setting up? But when they plugged in their equipment, something, like, happened? And now we, like, have no electricity?" Her pitch rose until she was positively squeaky. "And, like, the band can't play and the ice cream is going to melt and we haven't even served lunch yet and I'm, like, freaking out?"

Fiona pursed her lips. "You have a real problem," she said.

"I know!" Lucia exploded.

"Why don't you go ask one of your friends for help?" Fiona suggested. Her voice had a nasty edge.

"I . . ." Lucia looked hurt. "I *am*," she said.

Mitchie looked at me, and I knew she'd felt the same dagger in her heart that I had at Lucia's words. The only one who seemed unaffected was Fiona.

"I asked the others, too," Lucia admitted. "But none of them knew what to do."

A gloating smile started at the corners of Fiona's lips. She glanced at Mitchie as if she was about to say something smug.

But Mitchie just lifted her eyebrows. *What are you going to do about it?* her expression seemed to say.

Fiona blinked as if a thought had just occurred to her. She glanced at me, then turned to look at Lucia. The expression on Fiona's face had changed, as if she was seeing the desperate look on her friend's face for the first time. The nastiness that had crept into her blue eyes cleared. "Well . . . I guess . . . I guess the most important thing is not to panic," Fiona told her.

Lucia nodded. "Okay? Don't panic? Now what?"

"Tell Order by Numbers that they'll have to play unplugged — they'll do an acoustic set," Fiona instructed. "And we'll serve lunch in reverse. Ice cream first, before it melts."

"But the servers are, like, busy arranging the lunch plates?" Lucia said. "Who'll serve the ice cream?"

"I will," Fiona said.

Lucia grabbed her hand gratefully. "You will?"

I looked over at Mitchie, who nodded. "We'll help," I told her.

"Really?" Lucia looked shocked.

"What are friends for?" Fiona asked.

Lucia gaped at her for a moment, as if she was thinking over the question.

"Lead me to your mint chocolate chip," Mitchie said after a beat. Without a word, Lucia turned and led us across the lawn.

We were almost at the trellis when I heard someone shouting my name. Scott was waving at me and jogging over to join me. "I'll be there in a minute," I told Mitchie. She nodded and followed Lucia and Fiona to the ice-cream table.

"Hey." I flashed Scott a warm smile. "What's up?"

"I could ask you the same question," he said. He jerked his head toward Fiona. "I thought you

146

weren't going to hang out with those girls any-more." He folded his arms across his chest and gave me this weird little smile. It made me feel like I was about two years old.

Stay calm, I told myself. "Those girls are my friends," I said slowly.

"They don't know how to be friends — remember? *You* said that."

I thought that over for a moment. "I think maybe they're learning."

"They're just going to make you miserable." Scott's blondish hair looked golden in the bright sunshine, and his large brown eyes gleamed. He smiled at me with that bright, even smile. *He sure is handsome*, I thought.

I glanced over at the table where Mitchie and Lucia had started scooping out servings of ice cream. Fiona had organized lines and started tak-ing orders. Kiwi was handing out bowls. They were working together. And — okay — maybe Fiona wasn't perfect. None of my friends were per-fect. But that was all right because — guess what? I wasn't perfect, either.

Scott's perfect, I realized. *That's why he just doesn't get it.* And I didn't think he ever would.

"And when they make you miserable," Scott went on, "I don't want to hear any complaints about it." He waggled a finger at me and frowned disapprovingly. I think he was half kidding. On the other hand, that meant that he was half serious, too.

At that moment, I made a decision. I didn't want to go out on any more dates with Scott. I wasn't even sure I really wanted to be friends with him.

"Don't worry," I told him. "You won't."

"What's the scoop, Amy Flowers?" Preston asked.

"Chocolate," I told him as I ladled the soft ice cream into a bowl and handed it over.

Preston laughed. "Dessert just the way I like it," he said. "Before the main meal."

I chuckled, remembering the dinner I'd had with Scott. "You always know you'll have room for the sweet stuff," I teased.

"Hey, it's not like I eat like this every day."

"Thank goodness."

"You're one of the only people I know who could go to a party and end up working." He spooned up a mouthful of ice cream, then pointed at me with the empty spoon. "I'll bet you haven't even walked down to the ocean yet."

"You're right," I admitted. "I haven't."

"Well, Ms. Flowers . . ." Preston set down his bowl and held out a hand. "I suggest you take a break from your scooper."

"I can't —"

"Just for a minute." He tugged gently at my arm. "Come on, don't be boring."

"The people need their ice cream." I gestured toward the crowd gathered behind him. Actually, most of the crowd had already thinned out — there were only about five kids standing around, deciding on which flavor to have.

"Oh, go ahead," Mitchie said, bursting in on our conversation. "We've got it covered here."

Preston nodded at Fiona, Kiwi, and Jenelle. "You guys are a pretty efficient machine."

Mitchie saluted him with her scooper, and he laughed. Then — before I had a chance to take off the apron that Lucia had given me — he tugged my elbow and led me across the green lawn toward a tall dune. As we passed the small, spiky bushes on the clean golden sand, I heard the hiss and crash of the waves for the first time that day. We walked another ten feet to the top of the dune, and I looked down at the wide expanse of water. To my left, small waves lit with foam crashed against tall granite rocks. Preston headed the other way, where smooth sand stretched into the distance.

I pulled off my low-heeled sandals and waded through the soft dry sand. Closer to the water, the sand was firmer. The water, surprisingly warm, lapped up against my toes.

A wave crashed in, washing halfway up my calves. Preston swept his toes through the water in a kick, splashing me. With a shriek and a laugh, I splashed him back.

"Truce, truce!" he shouted as water dripped down his face. "This could easily get out of control."

"Like with the pudding?" I asked, remembering the time that Preston and I got into a fight with pistachio and vanilla homemade pudding.

"I'm not riding all the way back to Houston with wet, sandy shorts," Preston said.

"Yeah, the bus air-conditioning would probably give us pneumonia," I joked.

Our bare feet made perfect prints in the wet sand as we walked along the shore. Waves roared and crashed, then fizzed softly toward our toes. The sand gleamed for a moment before the water sank beneath its surface.

"So — you rescued Lucia's party," Preston said after a moment.

"Fiona was the real rescuer," I told him. "She was the one who came up with the plan."

Preston looked out over the horizon. "Yeah — Fiona can be cool sometimes," he said slowly. "It's just that sometimes she forgets how." He looked at me slyly out of the corner of his eye. "You can remind her."

"Like I know how to be cool," I joked.

Preston stopped and turned to face me. "You do," he said.

I laughed, then blushed. Preston didn't look away. A breeze kicked up, brushing his dark, shaggy hair away from his face. He looked down at me, and I realized that his green eyes were deeper than the sea.

My heart hammered through my chest. "So when are we going to Five Mountains?" I asked.

Omigosh, what did I just say? I thought as Preston smiled. *Did I just ask Preston out on a* date?

I think I did.

He reached out and tugged one of my curls, the way he had the other day. "Doink," he said quietly as the curl sprang back. I felt warm all over — my head was swimming. "What about Scott?"

I blinked up at him. "Who?" I asked. My tongue felt thick. I barely knew what I was saying; I'd forgotten how to form words. At that moment, I honestly didn't know what the word "Scott" meant.

Preston's grin widened. "What are you doing tomorrow?" he asked.

I felt like my smile had taken over my whole body — as if I was lit up from inside. I didn't know whether to laugh or jump in the water or fall over. But luckily, I didn't have to make a decision because at that moment I heard a war whoop. When I looked toward the top of the sand dune, I saw five figures racing toward us. Mitchie led the charge, followed by Anderson. Jenelle was on his heels, and so were Kiwi, and — trotting along daintily — Fiona.

"Get 'em!" Mitchie shouted, and she raced knee-high into the water and scooped a handful at Preston.

"Oooh, you're gonna get it!" he shouted, and he splashed Anderson.

In a moment, we were all splashing one another. Kiwi nailed me, and I got Jenelle. Fiona stood at the edge of the water.

"Anyone who gets me wet is dead," she announced.

Mitchie splashed her full in the face. For a moment, Fiona just looked shocked. Then a slow smile spread over her face. Her blue eyes gleamed. "Oh, it's *on*," she said.

Mitchie whooped and took off down the beach as Fiona tore after her. Mitchie screeched and giggled as Fiona flipped a small tidal wave toward her. Everyone got into the fray, shouting and laughing. Preston tackled Anderson and wrestled him into the sand.

So I guess we will all go back to Houston wet and sandy, I thought as I shot water across Kiwi's back. I didn't really think we'd get pneumonia, though.

Someone dumped water over my head. When I turned around, I came face-to-face with a grinning Fiona, and I realized that she looked happier than I'd ever seen her. It was a little shocking how well she fit in with the rest of my friends. I never would have thought it was possible. But I guess sometimes people surprise you. "How could you do that to me?" I wailed, teasing. "I thought we were friends!"

Fiona looked a little surprised, but her blue eyes were gleaming. Her black hair streamed out behind her on the breeze, and her dress fluttered.

"We are," she said at last.

CaNDY APPLE BOOKS

Read them all!

Accidentally
Fabulous

Accidentally
Famous

Accidentally
Fooled

Accidentally
Friends

How to Be a Girly Girl
in Just Ten Days

Miss Popularity

Miss Popularity
Goes Camping

Making Waves

Life, Starring Me!

Juicy Gossip

Callie for President

Totally Crushed